AT THE STILL POINT

A Literary Guide to Prayer in Ordinary Time

SARAH ARTHUR

At the Still Point: A Literary Guide to Prayer in Ordinary Time

ISBN 978-1-55725-785-7

The unattributed prayers found in Weeks 17 and 25 are by the author.

Library of Congress Cataloging-in-Publication Data
Arthur, Sarah.
At the still point : a literary guide to prayer in ordinary time / Sarah Arthur.
p. cm.
Includes bibliographical references (p.) and index.
ISBN 978-1-55725-785-7
1. Pentecost season—Prayers and devotions. 2. American literature.
3. English literature. I. Title.
BV61.A78 2011
242'.38--dc22
2011006180

10 9 8 7 6 5 4 3 2 1

Published by Paraclete Press
Brewster, Massachusetts
www.paracletepress.com
Printed in the United States of America

For our baby, Micah John,
whose conception, development, and birth
coincided with the creation of this book:
May you ever be
a lover of literature,
a haunter of libraries,
and a friend of Ordinary Time.

At the still point of the turning world. Neither flesh nor fleshless;
Neither from nor towards; at the still point, there the dance is…
—T. S. Eliot, from "Burnt Norton" in *Four Quartets*

CONTENTS

INTRODUCTION

THIS IS A GUIDE TO PRAYER FOR THE LITURGICAL SEASON KNOWN AS PENTECOST, OR ORDINARY TIME.[1] To my knowledge, however, it is not an ordinary guide to prayer. It does not contain readings from spiritual or devotional writings, discussing spiritual or devotional things through discursive thought. Rather, it is a journey of the imagination guided by poets and authors, both classic and contemporary, who have known the things of God but speak in metaphor. These are writers who tell the truth, as Emily Dickinson put it, but they "tell it slant." In not stating out loud what they know, they have left much to our imaginations—which is a way of saying they have trusted the Holy Spirit. *Let those who have ears, hear.*

For many Christians in the Northern Hemisphere, Ordinary Time coincides with summer and fall—a time that, for some of us, is far from ordinary. As a young child growing up in Michigan's northern lake country, I experienced summer as nothing short of miraculous, a kind of extended, intoxicating dream. After eight months of snow and ice and a muddy spring, school was finally out, strawberries were in, each body of water called for a sail or a swim. Sediments of sand piled up in the car and tub as we trekked daily from trail to dune, dune to shore, milking the warm sunlight while it lasted. Twilight was a world unto itself. We played outside till mosquitoes drove us indoors; and then we were sent to bed while it was still light enough to read, illegally, tilting the pages toward the fading light of the western windows till words ran together in the dark.

---

1 Two seasons of the church Year have periods of time that go by the name of "Ordinary Time." One occurs during the season between Epiphany and the beginning of Lent, and the other is the long stretch from Pentecost to Advent. This book focuses on the latter.

Dusk was the only time I read; the rest of my waking hours I played, hard, as if I had been given only four months to live. There seemed nothing ordinary about Ordinary Time. Years later I would scribble in a notebook, "I read poetry in springtime, novels in the winter, how-to books in autumn and baking recipes. But come summer, suddenly I'm somehow illiterate: creation itself is one long run-on sentence I can't find the end of." Finishing the thought with a preposition seemed to say it all. God was present in the summer, but not in finite words.

Then, sometime in my elementary years, my father, a Presbyterian minister, took his first pastorate in a farming community in central New York State. We lived between the two longest of the Finger Lakes, within ten minutes of cottage communities like the ones I remembered in Michigan. But the resort ethos did not extend up into the neighboring fields of corn and soy. Summertime meant labor and harvest for our community—and creeping boredom for us. What was a mother to do? Children underfoot all day, complaining, bored, in *summer*, of all times. Finally one morning she came home from running errands, carrying a stack of books. She had remembered, as good mothers often do, that entertainment and character formation do not have to be mutually exclusive, and both can be found at the local library. Two weeks later, my sister and I trooped along with her, and thus began a summer tradition.

That old library was a spectacular building, I realize now, converted from a colonial church with pillared columns and a wraparound balcony. The children's books and junior novels were in the lower level, in a kind of crypt with inset windows high in the walls, bookshelves from floor to ceiling. There I found treasures beyond reckoning, as one finds in cathedrals all over Europe, except these were words. To this day I associate libraries with old churches—which only makes sense, I suppose, for in both places one finds a quiet kind of reverence and "people of the book." And to this day I associate good books with ordinary summer days: bumblebees buzzing in the crypt windows; nothing much to do except crack open the cover of a library book (one that smells new, and you know you are the first to read it) and enter another world. Ordinary Time is reading time.

It is otherworldly time, a time when strange things happen, when tantalizing sounds waft to us from beyond the fields we know. It is a time when we are open to adventures, which is another way of saying that we are open to change. We remember certain scenes from certain books like we remember major life events: they become part of our personal histories, listed among the episodes that marked turning points in our lives. Indeed, many of us might include a poet or an author, whether dead or living, among our spiritual mentors. On a quiet evening, curled up with a good story, we have encountered the memorable character, the articulate phrase, the evocative image, the small suggestion, the smuggled truth, the shattering epiphany, which changed us, and we weren't even looking to be changed. It enriched our lives, and we didn't even know our own poverty. We were not the same people afterward.

Part of the power of such moments is that they sneak up on us when we are unaware. Spiritual insight, wrapped in the cloak of fiction or poetry, slips inside the back door of the imagination; and suddenly there it is, nonchalantly sipping coffee at the kitchen table. It pours another cup, invites us to have a seat. *Well,* it seems to say, *and what will you do with me now?* We were not expecting a spiritual moment because we didn't think we were reading a spiritual book. Our defenses were down. The bolt was unlocked. So the intruder gets further, pushes much deeper than if we, bristling with suspicion, had been expecting a salesman proselytizing at the front door.

Rather self-consciously, therefore, this book expands the genre of spiritual writing to include excerpts from classic and contemporary fiction and poetry, aimed at inviting you to experience God through your imagination. In these pages there are worlds to be explored, characters to meet, images to gaze upon, phrases to savor. This is back-door material, less interested in what you think than what you dream or feel. The applicability or relevance of these writings may not be immediately obvious, if ever. But, like parables, they can work on you over time, in your subconscious, perhaps surfacing later to offer unexpected insight, a slight shift in perspective.

Many of the authors whom I've included wrote in an attitude of Christian worship, even if the excerpt is not overtly Christian. And a few of the selections have been chosen in order to invite you to reflect Christianly, even if that is not what the original author might have intended. Together the readings create a rich (if not exhaustive) anthology that can draw you deeper into God's presence.

Of course, to collect such literary moments in a kind of anthology is to put the reader on high alert. These readings might as well come with neon signs saying, "Warning: Powerful Spiritual Moment Ahead"—which is tantamount to robbing them of all potential impact. By including these excerpts I do not insist that you be profoundly moved by each of them. Some will disappoint. Others will bewilder. What is a spiritual encounter for one person may not be for another.

For instance, I love the novels of Jane Austen. And yet, despite the fact that she was the daughter of a clergyman and wrote prayers for her household's evening devotions, it is a stretch to say that her novels are self-conscious acts of Christian worship. I will not inflict Elizabeth Bennet's epiphany, "Until this moment, I never knew myself," upon you, even if it has profound meaning for me. We must be careful, an English professor of mine once warned, not to "baptize" a literary work just because we happen to love it. A book may "baptize" our imaginations (in the words of C. S. Lewis), but we cannot turn, therefore, and become celebrants at the local library, pronouncing words of institution over every poem that delights us.

Even so, many of us have experienced a moment of spiritual awareness while reading a book that was not necessarily intended for that purpose. Like the apostle Paul, we have found ourselves atop a hill in Athens, conversing with Epicureans and Stoics, when suddenly struck by Christian truth issuing from the pen of a pagan poet. God has been at work in the world of books since long before there were such things as Christian publishing houses and Christian bookstores and Christian book groups. Indeed, God has been at work in the world of books since before there were Christians. As C. S. Lewis puts it, for many long centuries God sent humankind "good dreams"—ancient stories, legends, myths—that anticipated the work of God in Christ. The Holy Spirit has been known to use the secular for God's own purposes to an astonishing degree. And meanwhile, "A young man who wishes to remain a sound Atheist," writes Lewis, "cannot be too careful of his reading. There are traps everywhere—'Bibles laid open, millions of surprises,' as Herbert says, 'fine nets and stratagems.' God is, if I may say it, very unscrupulous."[2] If we thought we had entered the world of literature in order to be "safe" from divine interference, the Spirit is quite happy to take advantage of our wanderings.

---

2 C. S. Lewis, *Surprised by Joy: The Shape of My Early Life* (New York: Harcourt, 1955), 191.

So, be warned. Read on, reader. And meanwhile, keep in mind I am not suggesting that you stretch any of the readings in the direction that suits your current spiritual mood: otherwise the reading may break. However, I *am* inviting you to read these works differently than you might, say, for an English class or for personal entertainment. I'm inviting you to experience them as an act of worship, which was how many of the authors experienced or even intended them, and also as an opportunity for prayer, for conversation with God. I'm inviting you to read them like you read good books in summertime, at the beach or with the windows open, crickets buzzing in the sweet grass. Read like one who expects to be enchanted, at twilight, by the light of the first star. Because God is at work, not only in overtly spiritual things—devotionals and memoirs, liturgies and hymns—but also in the imaginative lives of God's people, in their subcreative worlds (as J.R.R. Tolkien put it), in their carefully crafted turns of phrase.

Here at the still point, in the nook at the top of the stairs, the Holy Spirit hovers, waiting, waiting for the sound of the turning page.

HOW TO USE THIS BOOK

The liturgical season of Ordinary Time runs for roughly twenty-nine weeks, from Pentecost Sunday in the spring until the first Sunday of Advent in late fall. It's the longest season of the church year, with few significant events along the way, which gives it a kind of ordinariness that the other seasons lack. There are no narrative highpoints, no showy colors or costumes, not even a signature hymn or two. Even the lectionary readings (or the cycle of Scriptures read by many denominations for each week of the church calendar), toil through lesser-known stories with a kind of plodding predictability. If Advent, Lent, and Easter are the glitzy celebrities at the liturgical party, Ordinary Time is the plain auntie collecting dirty wine glasses afterward. We almost forget she's there.

So to dress her up with some of the world's most extraordinary works of fiction and poetry is ironic, to say the least! But if, as the church prescribes, the season of Ordinary Time is when we are to focus on the mystery of Christ in *all* its aspects (not merely on the mystery of Christ's birth or resurrection, as in Advent and Easter), then this plain auntie just might surprise us. Seen in a slightly different light—say, emerging from the shadows into a moonlit garden—she might reveal something of the holy mystery that we hadn't seen before.

Think of the readings in this anthology as the moonlit garden. They are an invitation to experience the long season of Ordinary Time in a new way. To that end, they have been organized thematically, in groups of three to six, for each of the twenty-nine weeks; and their themes range all over the breadth of human spiritual experience: from conviction to calling, quarreling to awakening, dark nights, redemption, and everything in between. The weeks are not in chronological order to match the lectionary, so you are free to jump around. However, they *are* arranged with attention to the weeks that precede and follow them, so you may wish to follow the order given, just to see what the Spirit might spark in your imagination.

Each week begins with a suggested outline for daily prayer, including an opening and closing prayer, a psalm for the week, and suggested Scriptures. The psalm can be meditated upon daily, or you may wish to read only a portion of the psalm each day. Or find a particular section of the psalm with which you especially resonate and dwell there awhile, meditating on the words as a kind of personal prayer. The psalms as Hebrew poetry are some of the greatest literature you will encounter in a given week, providing echoes and resonances that a mere cursory skim will miss.

Meanwhile, both the Scriptures and the literary readings can be read daily or spread throughout the week as a guide for prayerful reflection. As you may already have discovered, the medium of poetry lends itself rather well to this kind of meditation. It is nearly impossible to read a poem both quickly and well. Often we find ourselves reading it a second or even a third time, savoring its images, marveling at the carefully crafted word patterns. It may not be all that difficult to imagine how to turn your poetic meditation into prayerful reflection, inviting God into your wonderings and insights.

But the fiction excerpts are a different matter. In many cases, you will be jumping in mid-story, with only a brief editor's note to orient you to people, places, and plot. It may take you a moment to settle in to the author's voice, to let the story weave its spell on your imagination. That's why some of the excerpts are rather long, because fiction doesn't work its magic right away. You might consider picking a day in the week in which you will focus only on the story excerpt, rather than trying to cram the other readings in as well. (However, not every week contains a fiction excerpt.) And meanwhile, you are absolved from trying to hunt for the story's "point." Some of the fiction may have obvious connections to the weekly theme; others may not. Rather than agonize over an excerpt, it is perfectly okay to move on, trusting that if the Spirit has something to say to you (whether it has to do with the theme or not), the insight will come in time.

If you desire to deepen your exploration of each week's themes, the back of the book includes a section titled "For Further Reading."

Still unsure of how to engage fiction or poetry prayerfully? Consider applying aspects of the practice of *lectio divina* (divine reading) to this process. It is an ancient method for prayerful meditation on the Scriptures, involving four steps: *lectio* (reading the passage), *meditatio* (meditating; reading it over several more times slowly), *oratio* (letting the text speak to you by paying attention to words, phrases, images, or ideas), and *contemplatio* (shifting one's focus to God; resting in God's presence). To be clear, I recognize that these literary readings are not the words of Scripture. So perhaps we might call this process *lectio sacra* (holy reading). Whatever the case, the basic principles of *lectio* that one might apply to Scripture can be applied to novels and poetry, since Scripture is in fact great literature. And meanwhile, as we have already noted, the Spirit is unscrupulous about means or method.

In the prayer outline for each day, you will notice there is an opportunity for personal prayer and reflection that follows the readings of Scripture and literature. This is the *oratio* and *contemplatio* stage. You have read the passage (*lectio*)—perhaps several times, slowly (*meditatio*)—and now you go back through it, making note of the words, phrases, images, metaphors, or ideas that "shimmer." What jumps out at you? What speaks to you (*oratio*)? You may even want to write it down. Then invite God to show you why this word or phrase spoke so strongly. What is God up to? In what ways do you sense God's presence in the midst of this reading? Finally, pause and simply rest in that presence (*contemplatio*). There are no demands on you in this moment. You are simply resting in God.

Here at the still point, read. Listen. Wonder.

Rest.

WEEK 1

Encountering the Spirit

OPENING PRAYER

Come Lord, Come Wisdom, Love, and Power,
  Open our ears to hear;
Let us not miss the accepted hour;
  Save, Lord, by Love or Fear.
—JOHN KEBLE (English, 1792–1866)

SCRIPTURES

PSALM 104 | JOEL 2:21–32 | ACTS 2:1–21 | JOHN 20:19–23

READINGS

"Not Like a Dove" by MARY F. C. PRATT
"God's Grandeur" by GERARD MANLEY HOPKINS
"A.M." by ROBERT SIEGEL
From *The Wind in the Willows* by KENNETH GRAHAME

PERSONAL PRAYER AND REFLECTION

CLOSING PRAYER

Listen sweet Dove unto my song,
And spread thy golden wings in me;
Hatching my tender heart so long,
Till it get wing, and fly away with thee.
—GEORGE HERBERT (English, 1593–1633)

READINGS FOR WEEK 1

Not Like a Dove

Mary F. C. Pratt (American, contemporary)

Come Holy Spirit, come
like a red eft[3] creeping out
from under wet leaves
crossing the traveled highway
at night after rain.
Come like the brown anole comes north
unexpected in bananas or limes;
like a gecko hunting roaches on a wall.
Come like Chameleon;
like Iguana still as deep green death
flittering a cloven tongue.
Come like Komodo parting the ways
with your stinking breath. Come
clear the carrion from this isle.
Come Holy Spirit
come like the Dragon remembered of old
rattling and clanking on golden wings.
Seize our treasures for your glittering hoard.
Burn away all that will burn.

God's Grandeur

Gerard Manley Hopkins (English, 1844–1889)

The world is charged with the grandeur of God.
    It will flame out, like shining from shook foil;

3 *eft*—a young newt

It gathers to a greatness, like the ooze of oil
Crushed. Why do men then now not reck his rod?
Generations have trod, have trod, have trod;
And all is seared with trade; bleared, smeared with toil;
And wears man's smudge and shares man's smell: the soil
Is bare now, nor can foot feel, being shod.

And for all this, nature is never spent;
There lives the dearest freshness deep down things;
And though the last lights off the black West went
Oh, morning, at the brown brink eastward, springs—
Because the Holy Ghost over the bent
World broods with warm breast and with ah! bright wings.

A.M.

ROBERT SIEGEL (American, contemporary)

Yellow flames flutter
about the feeder:
a Pentecost of finches.

FROM *The Wind in the Willows*

KENNETH GRAHAME (Scottish, 1859–1932)

[Editor's note: Grahame's classic children's book about the adventures of animal friends contains one of the most powerful scenes depicting a creature's response to the call of a holy "Other." In this scene, Rat and Mole are patrolling the river in search of a baby otter that has gone missing, when mysterious music wafts across the water. The longing that such music stirs in Rat, and the awe it produces in Mole, beautifully captures what an encounter with the Spirit (in this case the god Pan) does to the soul.]

Then a change began slowly to declare itself. The horizon became clearer, field and tree came more into sight, and somehow with a different look; the mystery began to drop away from them. A bird piped suddenly, and was still; and a light breeze sprang up and set the reeds and bulrushes rustling. Rat, who was in the stern of the boat, while Mole sculled, sat up suddenly and listened with a passionate intentness. Mole, who with gentle strokes was just keeping the boat moving while he scanned the banks with care, looked at him with curiosity.

"It's gone!" sighed the Rat, sinking back in his seat again. "So beautiful and strange and new! Since it was to end so soon, I almost wish I had never heard it. For it has roused a longing in me that is pain, and nothing seems worth while but just to hear that sound once more and go on listening to it for ever. No! There it is again!" he cried, alert once more. Entranced, he was silent for a long space, spell-bound.

"Now it passes on and I begin to lose it," he said presently. "O, Mole! the beauty of it! The merry bubble and joy, the thin, clear, happy call of the distant piping! Such music I never dreamed of, and the call in it is stronger even than the music is sweet! Row on, Mole, row! For the music and the call must be for us."

The Mole, greatly wondering, obeyed. "I hear nothing myself," he said, "but the wind playing in the reeds and rushes and osiers."

The Rat never answered, if indeed he heard. Rapt, transported, trembling, he was possessed in all his senses by this new divine thing that caught up his helpless soul and swung and dandled it, a powerless but happy infant in a strong sustaining grasp. . . .

"Clearer and nearer still," cried the Rat joyously. "Now you must surely hear it! Ah—at last—I see you do!"

Breathless and transfixed the Mole stopped rowing as the liquid run of that glad piping broke on him like a wave, caught him up, and possessed him utterly. He saw the tears on his comrade's cheeks, and bowed his head and understood. For a space they hung there, brushed by the purple loose-strife that fringed the bank; then the clear imperious summons that marched hand-in-hand with the intoxicating melody imposed its will on Mole, and mechanically he bent to his oars again. And the light grew steadily stronger, but no birds sang as they were wont to do at the approach of dawn; and but for the heavenly music all was marvellously still.

[continued below]

FROM *The Wind in the Willows*

Slowly, but with no doubt or hesitation whatever, and in something of a solemn expectancy, the two animals passed through the broken, tumultuous water and moored their boat at the flowery margin of the island. In silence they landed, and pushed through the blossom and scented herbage and undergrowth that led up to the level ground, till they stood on a little lawn of a marvellous green, set round with Nature's own orchard-trees—crab-apple, wild cherry, and sloe.

"This is the place of my song-dream, the place the music played to me," whispered the Rat, as if in a trance. "Here, in this holy place, here if anywhere, surely we shall find Him!"

Then suddenly the Mole felt a great Awe fall upon him, an awe that turned his muscles to water, bowed his head, and rooted his feet to the ground. It was no panic terror—indeed he felt wonderfully at peace and happy—but it was an awe that smote and held him and, without seeing, he knew it could only mean that some august Presence was very, very near. With difficulty he turned to look for his friend, and saw him at his side, cowed, stricken, and trembling violently. And still there was utter silence in the populous bird-haunted branches around them; and still the light grew and grew.

Perhaps he would never have dared to raise his eyes, but that, though the piping was now hushed, the call and the summons seemed still dominant and imperious. He might not refuse, were Death himself waiting to strike him instantly, once he had looked with mortal eye on things rightly kept hidden. Trembling he obeyed, and raised his humble head; and then, in that utter clearness of the imminent dawn, while Nature, flushed with fullness of incredible color, seemed to hold her breath for the event, he looked in the very eyes of the Friend and Helper; saw the backward sweep of the curved horns, gleaming in the growing daylight; saw the stern, hooked nose between the kindly eyes that were looking down on them humorously, while the bearded mouth broke into a half-smile at the corners; saw the rippling muscles on the arm that lay across the broad chest, the long supple hand still holding the pan-pipes only just fallen away from the parted lips; saw the splendid curves of the shaggy limbs disposed in majestic ease on the sward. . . . All this he saw, for one moment breathless and intense, vivid on the morning sky; and still, as he looked, he lived; and still, as he lived, he wondered.

"Rat!" he found breath to whisper, shaking. "Are you afraid?"

"Afraid?" murmured the Rat, his eyes shining with unutterable love. "Afraid! Of *Him*? O, never, never! And yet—and yet—O, Mole, I am afraid!"

Then the two animals, crouching to the earth, bowed their heads and did worship.

WEEK 2

In the Stillness

OPENING PRAYER

O Jesus! Who knows how much in Holy Scripture refers to peace of soul? Since, O my God, you see how important this peace is to us, incite Christians to strive to gain it. In your mercy do not deprive those on whom you have bestowed it, for until you have given them true peace and brought them to where it is unending, they must ever live in fear. —Teresa of Avila (Spanish, 1515–1582)

SCRIPTURES

Psalm 131 | Isaiah 26:1–9 | Philippians 4:4–7 | Matthew 6:1–6

READINGS

"Passing Ordinary Time" by Enuma Okoro
"A Song of Praises" by Robert Siegel
"Small Things" by Anna Kamieńska
"Earth's Crammed with Heaven" (excerpts from *Aurora Leigh*) by Elizabeth Barrett Browning

PERSONAL PRAYER AND REFLECTION

CLOSING PRAYER

Still may thy sweet mercy spread
A shady arm above my head,
About my paths, so shall I find
The fair Center of my mind
Thy Temple, and those lovely walls

Bright ever with a beam that falls
Fresh from the pure glance of thine eye,
Lighting to Eternity.
—RICHARD CRASHAW (English,1613–1649)

READINGS FOR WEEK 2

Passing Ordinary Time

ENUMA OKORO (Nigerian-American, contemporary)

It is a hard art to learn,
catching quiet
by palms raised
cupped in
air shifting location
here and there like
trying to guess the pattern of falling leaves,
and hoping to feel
the soft descent of moments
when silence slips
between sounds.

This ordinary time is
gifted with days,
weeks of mundane grace
routinely following the liturgy
of hours anticipating creation
tuning its prayer and praise to the
rhythms of incarnate love.

I am used to the uproar,
the Holy drama,

the appetite's gnarled discord
of fasting and feasting on borrowed time,
the knocking of angels,
the blubbering piety of waiting,
appointed seasons for guilt and grief,
tears of joy and disbelief,
the birth of miracles, the passion of virgins,
the mourning of a love so divine.

This ordinary time is
gifted in its quiet, marked passing
Christ slips about
calling and baptizing,
sending and affirming,
pouring his Spirit like water
into broken cisterns,
sealing cracks and filtering our senses,
that we may savor the foolish
simplicity of his grace.

A Song of Praises

ROBERT SIEGEL (American, contemporary)

for the gray nudge of dawn at the window
for the chill that hangs around the bed and slips
  its cold tongue under the covers
for the cat who walks over my face purring murderously
for the warmth of the hip next to mine and sweet lethargy
for the cranking up of the will until it turns me out of bed
for the robe's caress along arm and neck
for the welcome of hot water, the dissolving of
  the night's stiff mask in the warm washcloth

for the light along the white porcelain sink
for the toothbrush's savory invasion of the tomb of the mouth
  and resurrection of the breath
for the warm lather and the clean scrape of the razor
  and the skin smooth and pink that emerges
for the steam of the shower, the apprehensive shiver and then
  its warm enfolding of the shoulders
  its falling on the head like grace
  its anointing of the whole body
  and the soap's smooth absolution
for the rough nap of the towel and its message to each skin cell
for the hairbrush's pulling and pulling,
  waking the root of each hair
for the reassuring snap of elastic
for the hug of the belt that pulls all together

for the smell of coffee rising up the stairs announcing paradise
for the glass of golden juice in which light is condensed
  and the grapefruit's sweet flesh
for the incense of butter on toast
for the eggs like two peaks over which the sun rises
  and the jam for which the strawberries of summer have
  saved themselves

for the light whose long shaft lifts the kitchen
  into the realms of day
for Mozart elegantly measuring out the gazebos
  of heaven on the radio
and for her face, for whom the kettle sings, the coffee percs,
  and all the yellow birds in the wallpaper spread their wings.

———

Small Things

ANNA KAMIEŃSKA (Polish, 1920–1986)

It usually starts taking shape
from one word
reveals itself in one smile
sometimes in the blue glint of eyeglasses
in a trampled daisy
in a splash of light on a path
in quivering carrot leaves
in a bunch of parsley
It comes from laundry hung on a balcony
from hands thrust into dough
It seeps through closed eyelids
as through the prison wall of things of objects
of faces of landscapes
It's when you slice bread
when you pour out some tea
It comes from a broom from a shopping bag
from peeling new potatoes
from a drop of blood from the prick of a needle
when making panties for a child
or sewing a button on a husband's burial shirt
It comes out of toil out of care
out of immense fatigue in the evening
out of a tear wiped away
out of a prayer broken off in mid-word by sleep

It's not from the grand
but from every tiny thing
that it grows enormous
as if Someone was building Eternity
as a swallow its nest
out of clumps of moments

"Earth's Crammed with Heaven"

(EXCERPTS FROM *Aurora Leigh*, Book VII)

ELIZABETH BARRETT BROWNING (English, 1806–1861)

. . . For the truth itself,
That's neither man's nor woman's, but just God's;
None else has reason to be proud of truth:
Himself will see it sifted, disenthralled,
And kept upon the height and in the light,
As far as, and no farther, than 'tis truth;
For,—now He has left off calling firmaments
And strata, flowers and creatures, very good,—
He says it still of truth, which is His own.
Truth, so far, in my book;—the truth which draws
Through all things upwards; that a twofold world
Must go to a perfect cosmos. Natural things
And spiritual,—who separates those two
In art, in morals, or the social drift,
Tears up the bond of nature and brings death,
Paints futile pictures, writes unreal verse,
Leads vulgar days, deals ignorantly with men,
Is wrong, in short, at all points. We divide
This apple of life, and cut it through the pips,—
The perfect round which fitted Venus' hand
Has perished utterly as if we ate
Both halves. Without the spiritual, observe,
The natural's impossible;—no form,
No motion! Without sensuous, spiritual
Is inappreciable;—no beauty or power!
And in this twofold sphere the twofold man
(And still the artist is intensely a man)
Holds firmly by the natural, to reach
The spiritual beyond it,—fixes still

The type with mortal vision, to pierce through,
With eyes immortal, to the antitype
Some call the ideal,—better called the real,
And certain to be called so presently,
When things shall have their names. . . .

[continued below]

"Earth's Crammed with Heaven"

. . . An artist must,
Who paints a tree, a leaf, a common stone
With just his hand, and finds it suddenly
A-piece with and conterminous to his soul.
Why else do these things move him, leaf or stone?
The bird's not moved, that pecks at a spring-shoot;
Nor yet the horse, before a quarry, a-graze:
But man, the two-fold creature, apprehends
The two-fold manner, in and outwardly,
And nothing in the world comes single to him.
A mere itself,–cup, column, or candlestick,
All patterns of what shall be in the Mount;
The whole temporal show related royally,
And build up to eternal significance
Through the open arms of God. 'There's nothing great
Nor small,' has said a poet of our day,
(Whose voice will ring beyond the curfew of eve
And not be thrown out by the matins' bell)
And truly, I reiterate, . . . nothing's small!
No lily-muffled hum of a summer-bee,
But finds some coupling with the spinning stars;
No pebble at your foot, but proves a sphere;
No chaffinch, but implies the cherubim:

And,–glancing on my own thin, veined wrist,–
In such a little tremor of the blood
The whole strong clamor of a vehement soul
Doth utter itself distinct. Earth's crammed with heaven,
And every common bush afire with God:
But only he who sees, takes off his shoes,
The rest sit round it, and pluck blackberries,
And daub their natural faces unaware
More and more, from the first similitude.

WEEK 3

The Other Side of Silence

OPENING PRAYER

Be not thou silent now at length,
O God hold not thy peace,
Sit not thou still O God of strength,
We cry and do not cease.
—JOHN MILTON (English, 1608–1674)

SCRIPTURES

PSALM 83 | 1 KINGS 19:1–13a | REVELATION 8:1–6 | LUKE 1:5–23

READINGS

"The Three Silences . . . " by HENRY WADSWORTH LONGFELLOW
"Mute" by ELIZABETH B. ROONEY
"Subliminal messages" by LUCI SHAW
"Substitution" by ELIZABETH BARRETT BROWNING
From *Middlemarch* by GEORGE ELIOT

PERSONAL PRAYER AND REFLECTION

CLOSING PRAYER

My prayers, my God, flow from what I am not;
I think thy answers make me what I am.
Like weary waves thought follows upon thought,
But the still depth beneath is all thine own,
And there thou mov'st in paths to us unknown.
Out of strange strife thy peace is strangely wrought;
If the lion in us pray—thou answerest the lamb.
—GEORGE MACDONALD (Scottish, 1824–1905)

READINGS FOR WEEK 3

The Three Silences . . .

HENRY WADSWORTH LONGFELLOW (American, 1807–1882)

Three Silences there are: the first of speech,
The second of desire, the third of thought;
This is the lore a Spanish monk, distraught
With dreams and visions, was the first to teach.
These Silences, commingling each with each,
Made up the perfect Silence, that he sought
And prayed for, and wherein at times he caught
Mysterious sounds from realms beyond our reach.
O thou, whose daily life anticipates
The life to come, and in whose thought and word
The spiritual world preponderates,
Hermit of Amesbury! thou too hast heard
Voices and melodies from beyond the gates,
And speakest only when thy soul is stirred!

———

Mute

Elizabeth B. Rooney (American, 1924–1999)

Must we use words
For everything?
Can there not be
A silent, flaming
Leap of heart
Toward Thee?

Subliminal messages

Luci Shaw (Naturalized U.S. Citizen, contemporary)

The telephone is silent; God doesn't return
  my calls to the office.
We're supposed to be married, but I think
  he's left me, gone
on a long trip to the Antarctic—somewhere
  cold.
The pleading letters I write him pile up,
  unsent, on the hall table;
I have no forwarding address for declarations
  of desire, invitations
to come back to me, flowers, a new book,
  a birthday present in December.
Living in the dumbness of a dead phone, an
  empty mailbox,
always, when I get home from work, the house
  is dark, the dog bored,
the plants browning, the sink piled with
  my own dirty dishes.

But yesterday the sun came out for half
  an hour, whitening the curtains
from outside. Maybe it was a message,
  subliminal,
like the Two Part Inventions on the car
  radio
with Bach's questions and answers—two voices
  in conversation,
or the way the wind strokes the roof
  at night
or the rain tracks down the window glass,
  intimate as tears.

Substitution

ELIZABETH BARRETT BROWNING (English, 1806–1861)

When some beloved voice that was to you
Both sound and sweetness, faileth suddenly,
And silence, against which you dare not cry,
Aches round you like a strong disease and new—
What hope? what help? what music will undo
That silence to your sense? Not friendship's sigh,
Not reason's subtle count; not melody
Of viols, nor of pipes that Faunus blew;
Not songs of poets, nor of nightingales
Whose hearts leap upward through the cypress-trees
To the clear moon; nor yet the spheric laws
Self-chanted, nor the angels' sweet 'All hails,'
Met in the smile of God: nay, none of these.
Speak THOU, availing Christ!—and fill this pause.

FROM *Middlemarch*

GEORGE ELIOT (a.k.a., Mary Anne Evans; English, 1819–1880)

[Editor's note: One of Eliot's most memorable characters is young Dorothea Brooke, whose desire to live a noble, intellectual, and serviceable life has led her to marry (rather unwisely) the much older Rev. Casaubon. While he is doing research in Rome for an ongoing theological project, Dorothea wanders alone from landmark to landmark, an experience of silence and solitude that forces her to reflect on the future that now faces her.]

To those who have looked at Rome with the quickening power of a knowledge which breathes a growing soul into all historic shapes, and traces out the suppressed transitions which unite all contrasts, Rome may still be the spiritual center and interpreter of the world. But let them conceive one more historical contrast: the gigantic broken revelations of that Imperial and Papal city thrust abruptly on the notions of a girl who had been brought up in English and Swiss Puritanism, fed on meager Protestant histories and on art chiefly of the hand-screen sort; a girl whose ardent nature turned all her small allowance of knowledge into principles, fusing her actions into their mould, and whose quick emotions gave the most abstract things the quality of a pleasure or a pain; a girl who had lately become a wife, and from the enthusiastic acceptance of untried duty found herself plunged in tumultuous preoccupation with her personal lot. The weight of unintelligible Rome might lie easily on bright nymphs to whom it formed a background for the brilliant picnic of Anglo-foreign society; but Dorothea had no such defense against deep impressions. Ruins and basilicas, palaces and colossi, set in the midst of a sordid present, where all that was living and warm-blooded seemed sunk in the deep degeneracy of a superstition divorced from reverence; the dimmer but yet eager Titanic life gazing and struggling on walls and ceilings; the long vistas of white forms whose marble eyes seemed to hold the monotonous light of an alien world: all this vast wreck of ambitious ideals, sensuous and spiritual, mixed confusedly with the signs of breathing forgetfulness and degradation, at first jarred her as with an electric shock, and then urged themselves on her with that ache belonging to a glut of confused ideas which check the flow of emotion. Forms both pale and glowing took possession of her young sense, and fixed themselves in her memory even when she was not thinking of them, preparing strange associations which remained through her after-years. Our moods are apt to bring with them images which succeed each other like the magic-lantern pictures of a doze; and in certain states of dull forlornness Dorothea all her life continued to see the vastness of St. Peter's, the huge bronze canopy, the excited intention in the attitudes and garments of the prophets and evangelists in the mosaics above, and the red drapery which was being hung for Christmas spreading itself everywhere like a disease of the retina.

Not that this inward amazement of Dorothea's was anything very exceptional: many souls in their young nudity are tumbled out among incongruities and left "to find their feet" among them, while their elders go about their business. Nor can I suppose that when Mrs. Casaubon is discovered in a fit of weeping six weeks after her wedding, the situation will be regarded as tragic. Some discouragement, some faintness of heart at the new real future which replaces the imaginary, is not unusual, and we do not expect people to be deeply moved by what is not unusual. That element of tragedy which lies in the very fact of frequency, has not yet wrought itself into the coarse emotion of mankind; and perhaps our frames could hardly bear much of it. If we had a keen vision and feeling of all ordinary human life, it would be like hearing the grass grow and the squirrel's heart beat, and we should die of that roar which lies on the other side of silence. As it is, the quickest of us walk about well wadded with stupidity.

WEEK 4

Seeking God's Face

OPENING PRAYER

O may my soul, uncrushed by care,
Direct her gaze to where Thou art,
And in Thy splendor find, O Christ,
The strength of life Thou canst impart.
—adapted from the poetry of Synesius
(Greek, AD 375–430)

SCRIPTURES

Psalm 84 | 1 Kings 8:22–30 | Colossians 1:3–10 | Luke 11:1–8

READINGS

"Prayer (I)" by George Herbert
"Divina Commedia (I)" by Henry Wadsworth Longfellow
"The Prayers" by Thomas Edward Brown
From *Diary of an Old Soul* by George MacDonald
From *At the Back of the North Wind* by George MacDonald

PERSONAL PRAYER AND REFLECTION

CLOSING PRAYER

May my soul, her want perceiving,
Turn her gaze to where Thou art,
And in all Thy fullness find Thee
Food to satisfy the heart.
—adapted from the poetry of Synesius
(Greek, AD 375–430)

READINGS FOR WEEK 4

Prayer (I)

George Herbert (English, 1593–1633)

Prayer the Church's banquet, Angels' age,
God's breath in man returning to his birth,
The soul in paraphrase, heart in pilgrimage,
The Christian plummet sounding heav'n and earth;
Engine against th' Almighty, sinners' tower,
Reversed thunder, Christ-side-piercing spear,
The six-days world transposing in an hour,
A kind of tune, which all things hear and fear;
Softness, and peace, and joy, and love, and bliss,
Exalted Manna, gladness of the best,
Heaven in ordinary, man well dressed,
The milky way, the bird of Paradise,
Church-bells beyond the stars heard, the soul's blood,
The land of spices; something understood.

Divina Commedia (I)

Henry Wadsworth Longfellow (American, 1807–1882)

Oft have I seen at some cathedral door
A laborer, pausing in the dust and heat,
Lay down his burden, and with reverent feet
Enter, and cross himself, and on the floor
Kneel to repeat his paternoster o'er;
Far off the noises of the world retreat;
The loud vociferations of the street

Become an undistinguishable roar.
So, as I enter here from day to day,
And leave my burden at this minster gate,
Kneeling in prayer, and not ashamed to pray,
The tumult of the time disconsolate
To inarticulate murmurs dies away,
While the eternal ages watch and wait.

The Prayers

THOMAS EDWARD BROWN (British, 1830–1897)

I was in Heaven one day when all the prayers
Came in, and angels bore them up the stairs
Unto a place where he
Who was ordained such ministry
Should sort them so that in that palace bright
The presence-chamber might be duly dight;[4]
For they were like to flowers of various bloom;
And a divinest fragrance filled the room.

Then did I see how the great sorter chose
One flower that seemed to me a hedgeling rose,
And from the tangled press
Of that irregular loveliness
Set it apart—and "This," I heard him say,
"Is for the Master": so upon his way
He would have passed; then I to him:—
"Whence is this rose? O thou of cherubim
The chiefest?"—"Know'st thou not?" he said and smiled,
"This is the first prayer of a little child."

---

4 *dight*—adorned or dressed.

From *Diary of an Old Soul*

George MacDonald (Scottish, 1824–1905)

I see a child before an empty house,
Knocking and knocking at the closed door;
He wakes dull echoes—but nor man nor mouse,
If he stood knocking there forevermore.
A mother angel, see, folding each wing,
Soft-walking, crosses straight the empty floor,
And opens to the obstinate praying thing.

From *At the Back of the North Wind*

George MacDonald (Scottish, 1824–1905)

[Editor's note: In MacDonald's most famous children's book, a little boy named Diamond discovers that the cold wind blowing outside his hayloft bedroom is in fact a personality. At first he encounters only her voice, but soon he will see the North Wind face-to-face. Diamond is both terrified and drawn to her, and then agrees to follow her—a lovely image of childlike faith.]

"I am the North Wind."

"O-o-oh!" said Diamond thoughtfully. "Then will you promise not to blow on my face if I open your window?"

"I can't promise that."

"But you'll give me a toothache. Mother's got it already."

"But what's to become of me without a window?"

"I'm sure I don't know. All I say is, it will be worse for me than for you."

"No; it will not. You shall not be the worse for it, I promise you that. You will be much the better for it. Just you believe what I say, and do as I tell you."

"Well, I *can* pull the clothes over my head," said Diamond, and feeling with his little sharp nails, he got hold of the open edge of the paper and tore it off at once.

In came a long whistling spear of cold, and struck his little naked chest. He scrambled and tumbled in under the bedclothes, and covered himself up. . . .

. . . "Will you take your head out of the bedclothes?" said the voice, just a little angrily.

"No!" answered Diamond, half peevish, half frightened.

The instant he said the word a tremendous blast of wind crashed in a board of the wall, and swept the clothes off Diamond. He started up in terror. Leaning over him was the large beautiful pale face of a woman. Her dark eyes looked a little angry for they had just begun to flash; but a quivering in her sweet upper lip made her look as if she were going to cry. What was most strange was that away from her head streamed out her black hair in every direction, so that the darkness in the hay-loft looked as if it were made of her hair; but as Diamond gazed at her in speechless amazement, mingled with confidence—for the boy was entranced with her mighty beauty—her hair began to gather itself out of the darkness, and fell down all about her again, till her face looked out of the midst of it like a moon out of a cloud. From her eyes came all the light by which Diamond saw her face and her hair; and that was all he did see of her yet. The wind was over and gone.

"Will you go with me now, you little Diamond? I am sorry I was forced to be so rough with you," said the lady.

"I will; yes, I will," answered Diamond, holding out both his arms. "But," he added, dropping them, "how shall I get my clothes? They are in Mother's room, and the door is locked."

"Oh, never mind your clothes. You will not be cold. I shall take care of that. Nobody is cold with the North Wind."

"I thought everybody was," said Diamond.

"That is a great mistake. Most people make it, however. They are cold because they are not with the North Wind, but without it."

If Diamond had been a little older, and had supposed himself a good deal wiser, he would have thought the lady was joking. But he was not older, and did not fancy himself wiser, and therefore understood her well enough. Again he stretched out his arms. The lady's face drew back a little.

[continued below]

FROM *At the Back of the North Wind*

"Follow me, Diamond," she said.

"Yes," said Diamond only a little ruefully.

"You're not afraid?" said the North Wind.

"No, ma'am" . . .

. . . "You're not to call me *ma'am*. You must call me just my own name—respectfully, you know—just North Wind."

"Well, please, North Wind, you are so beautiful, I am quite ready to go with you."

"You must not be ready to go with everything beautiful all at once, Diamond."

"But what's beautiful can't be bad. You're not bad, North Wind?"

"No; I'm not bad. But sometimes beautiful things grow bad by doing bad, and it takes some time for their badness to spoil their beauty. So little boys may be mistaken if they go after things because they are beautiful."

"Well, I will go with you because you are beautiful and good too."

"Ah, but there's another thing, Diamond: what if I should look ugly without being bad—look ugly myself because I am making ugly things beautiful? What then?"

"I don't quite understand you, North Wind. You tell me what then."

"Well, I will tell you. If you see me with my face all black, don't be frightened. If you see me flapping wings like a bat's, as big as the whole sky, don't be frightened. If you hear me raging ten times worse than Mrs. Bill, the blacksmith's wife—even if you see me looking in at people's windows like Mrs. Eve Dropper, the gardener's wife—you must believe that I am doing my work. Nay, Diamond, if I change into a serpent or a tiger, you must not let go your hold of me, for my hand will never change in yours if you keep a good hold. If you keep a hold, you will know who I am all the time, even when you look at me and can't see me the least like the North Wind. I may look something very awful. Do you understand?"

"Quite well," said little Diamond.

"Come along, then," said the North Wind, and disappeared behind the mountain of hay.

Diamond crept out of bed and followed her.

WEEK 5

The Intimacy of Grace

OPENING PRAYER

When You regarded me,
Your eyes imprinted in me Your grace:
For this You loved me again,
And thereby my eyes merited
To adore what in You they saw.
—JOHN OF THE CROSS (Spanish, 1542–1591)

SCRIPTURES

PSALM 116 | ISAIAH 40:1–11, 27–31 | ROMANS 8:26–30
JOHN 17:15–26

READINGS

"Later Life: A Double Sonnet of Sonnets (V)" by CHRISTINA ROSSETTI
"Comfort" by ELIZABETH BARRETT BROWNING
"Live to Love" by MADAME GUYON
The Loveliest Rose in the World by HANS CHRISTIAN ANDERSEN

PERSONAL PRAYER AND REFLECTION

CLOSING PRAYER

I praise Thee while my days go on;
I love Thee while my days go on:
Through dark and dearth, through fire and frost,
With emptied arms and treasure lost,
I thank Thee while my days go on.
—ELIZABETH BARRETT BROWNING (English, 1806–1861)

READINGS FOR WEEK 5

Later Life: A Double Sonnet of Sonnets (V)

Christina Rossetti (English, 1830–1894)

Lord, Thou Thyself art Love and only Thou;
Yet I who am not love would fain love Thee;
But Thou alone being Love canst furnish me
With that same love my heart is craving now.
Allow my plea! for if Thou disallow,
No second fountain can I find but Thee;
No second hope or help is left to me,
No second anything, but only Thou.
O Love accept, according my request;
O Love exhaust, fulfilling my desire:
Uphold me with the strength that cannot tire,
Nerve me to labor till Thou bid me rest,
Kindle my fire from Thine unkindled fire,
And charm the willing heart from out my breast.

Comfort

Elizabeth Barrett Browning (English, 1806–1861)

Speak low to me, my Savior, low and sweet
From out the hallelujahs, sweet and low
Lest I should fear and fall, and miss Thee so
Who art not missed by any that entreat.
Speak to me as to Mary at thy feet!
And if no precious gems my hands bestow,

Let my tears drop like amber while I go
In reach of thy divinest voice complete
In humanest affection—thus, in sooth,
To lose the sense of losing. As a child,
Whose song-bird seeks the wood for evermore
Is sung to in its stead by mother's mouth
Till, sinking on her breast, love-reconciled,
He sleeps the faster that he wept before.

Live to Love

MADAME GUYON (French, 1648–1717)

Since Life in sorrow must be spent,
So be it—I am well content,
And meekly wait my last Remove,
Seeking only growth in Love.

No bliss I seek but to fulfill
In life, in death, Thy lovely will,
No succor in my woes I want,
Save what Thou art pleased to grant.

Our days are numbered, let us spare
Our anxious hearts a needless care,—
'Tis Thine to number out our days,
Ours to give them to Thy praise.

Love is our only business here,
Love, simple, constant and sincere,
Oh blessed days Thy servants see,
Spent O Lord, in pleasing Thee!

The Loveliest Rose in the World

HANS CHRISTIAN ANDERSEN (Danish, 1805–1875)

[Editor's note: In this complete short story, Andersen blends the genres of fairytale and allegory to create a kind of parable that echoes the kingdom parables of Jesus (see Matt. 13:44–46). Andersen's moral is elegantly simple: God's intimate, self-giving love is the only thing that can heal the soul.]

There lived once a great queen, in whose garden were found at all seasons the most splendid flowers, and from every land in the world. She especially loved roses, and she owned the most beautiful kinds of this flower, from the wild hedge-rose, with its apple-scented leaves, to the splendid Provence rose. They grew near the shelter of the walls, wound themselves around columns and window-frames, crept along passages and over the ceilings of the halls. They were of every fragrance and color.

But worry and sorrow lived within these halls, because the queen lay sick, and the doctors said that she would die. "There is still one thing that could save her," said one of the wisest among them. "Bring her the loveliest rose in the world; one which shows the purest and brightest love. If it is brought to her before her eyes close, she will not die."

Then from all parts came those who brought roses that bloomed in every garden, but they were not the right kind. The flower must be one from the garden of love, but which of the roses there showed the highest and purest love? The poets sang of this rose, the loveliest in the world, and each named one which he considered worthy of that title. The request for such a rose was sent far and wide to every heart that beat with love; to every class, age, and condition.

"No one has yet named the flower," said the wise man. "No one has pointed out the spot where it blooms in all its splendor. It is not a rose from the coffin of young lovers, or from the grave of a hero who died for his country. Neither is it the magic flower of Science, obtained by a man who devotes many hours of his life in sleepless nights, in a lonely chamber."

"I know where it blooms," said a happy mother, who came with her lovely child to the bedside of the queen. "I know where the loveliest rose in the world is. It is seen on the blooming cheeks of my sweet child, when it is refreshed by sleep and opens its eyes to smile on me with love."

"This is a lovely rose," said the wise man, "but there is one still more lovely."

"Yes, one far more lovely," said one of the women. "I have seen it, and a grander and purer rose does not bloom. But it was white, like the leaves of a blush-rose. I saw it on the cheeks of the queen. She had taken off her golden crown, and through the long, dreary night, she carried her sick child in her arms. She wept over it, kissed it, and prayed for it as only a mother can pray in that hour of her suffering."

"Holy and wonderful is the white rose of grief, but it is not the one we seek."

"No, the loveliest rose in the world I saw at the Lord's table," said the good old minister. "I saw it shine as if an angel's face had appeared. A young maiden knelt at the altar and renewed the vows made at her baptism. And there were white roses and red roses on the blushing cheeks of that young girl. She looked up to heaven with an expression of the highest and purest love."

"May she be blessed!" said the wise man. "But no one has yet named the loveliest rose in the world."

Then there came into the room a child—the queen's little son. Tears stood in his eyes and glistened on his cheeks. He carried a great book covered in velvet, with silver clasps. "Mother," cried the little boy, "hear what I have read." And the child seated himself by the bedside, and read from the book about Him who suffered death on the cross to save all people, even who are yet unborn. He read, "Greater love has no man than this," and as he read a rosy color spread over the cheeks of the queen. Her eyes became so bright and clear that she saw a lovely rose spring out of the pages of the book—a sign of Him who shed His blood on the cross.

"I see it," she said. "He who beholds this, the loveliest rose on earth, shall never die."

WEEK 6

Sharing Burdens

OPENING PRAYER

Heal then these waters, Lord; or bring thy flock,
Since these are troubled, to the springing rock.
Look down, great Master of the Feast! O shine,
And turn once more our water into wine.
—HENRY VAUGHAN (Welsh, 1622–1695)

SCRIPTURES

PSALM 102 | I KINGS 17:17–24 | JAMES 5:13–18 | MARK 9:14–29

READINGS

"As the couple turn toward each other" by MARK JARMAN
"Prayer (II)" by GEORGE HERBERT
From *Peace Like a River* by LEIF ENGER

PERSONAL PRAYER AND REFLECTION

CLOSING PRAYER

Watch by the sick: enrich the poor
With blessings from Thy boundless store:
Be every mourner's sleep to-night,
Like infants' slumbers, pure and light.
—JOHN KEBLE (English, 1792–1866)

READINGS FOR WEEK 6

As the couple turn toward each other

MARK JARMAN (American, contemporary)

As the couple turn toward each other in the dark, without speaking; as the impulse to kiss the man or woman beside you is restrained; as a voice on the telephone slowly brings a face to mind; so prayer commences, strangely intimate with everything it thinks of.

Ed Bryant has rejected his new kidney. Sally Rogers, a friend of Missy Edwards, begins chemotherapy this week. Robert Powers, our janitor, is resting comfortably at home. The Niederthals and their children are still waiting permission to leave Tunisia. Hal Anderson is stuck on the tarmac in Detroit. Longtime executive director of the Sunday School Board, Erlise Hopson, was found in the bathroom of her apartment at the Millicent Christian Retirement Center. Let us also remember the Kurdish separatists in Turkey and Iraq.

Prayer aligns us with random forces. It is an impulse among impulses. It is like shining a flashlight into the night sky in your backyard. The light from prayer diverges, so its intensity (the flux per unit area) grows weaker the farther it goes. Mainly prayer is scattered (dispersed in new directions, if you like) by other prayers. In urban settings, there are lots of them in the atmosphere, and they deflect each other toward different ends. And yet our prayer heads into space, full of presumption that the speed of light will carry it beyond the Pleiades.

He sweated blood. He knew he was going to die. He prayed. He sweated, not blood but drops like blood. Arterial. Pulsing. As if to sweat this way might kill him. He could see how he would die and asked not to die. The one to whom he prayed answered with silence. Clasped by a hand of silence, at the end of an arm of silence, it was a cup of silence, holding the countless counted beads of his unanswered answered prayer.

So your face burns when you say, "I'll pray for you." So you believe a signal bounces off eternity and strikes the object of your prayer, and you blush to believe it, that is, to say so in so many words.

For it is as if in the presence of one we worked with daily and respected, with whom we spoke in familiar yet businesslike tones about matters of concern—writing reports, making proposals—a scene as formalized as liturgy presented us to one another naked. Or it is as if in the presence of one we loved, who would willingly undress for us, we pictured another life, in another place, with someone else.

I understand your reaction. *My* face burns.

I'll pray for you. I'll eat for you. I'll drink for you. I'll speak for you. I'll breathe for you. I'll write for you. I'll call for you. I'll work for you. I'll sing for you. I'll play for you. I'll live for you. I'll die for you. I'll change for you. I will speak to the nonexistent about your existence. I will add my impotence to your impotence.

And yet if everything prayed one prayer, it would have to be heard, wouldn't it? Perhaps that prayer is *Let me be*. That prayer is heard.

———

Prayer (II)

George Herbert (English, 1593–1633)

Of what an easy quick access,
My blessed Lord, art thou! how suddenly
May our requests thine ear invade!
To show that state dislikes not easiness,
If I but lift mine eyes, my suit is made:
Thou canst no more not hear, than thou canst die.

Of what supreme almighty power
Is thy great arm which spans the east and west,
And tacks the center to the sphere!
By it do all things live their measured hour:
We cannot ask the thing, which is not there,
Blaming the shallowness of our request.

Of what unmeasurable love
Art thou possessed, who, when thou couldst not die,
Wert fain to take our flesh and curse,
And for our sakes in person sin reprove,
That by destroying that which tied thy purse,
Thou mightst make way for liberality!

Since then these three wait on thy throne,
Ease, *Power*, and *Love*; I value prayer so,
That were I to leave all but one,
Wealth, fame, endowments, virtues, all should go;
I and dear prayer would together dwell,
And quickly gain, for each inch lost, an ell.

FROM *Peace Like a River*

LEIF ENGER (American, contemporary)

[Editor's note: The opening pages of Enger's contemporary novel set the stage for the unique father-son relationships that anchor the book. This will not be the last time Reuben's father prays prophetically, burdened for one of his children—nor will it be the last time his prayers lead to miracle.]

When I was born to Helen and Jeremiah Land, in 1951, my lungs refused to kick in.

My father wasn't in the delivery room or even in the building; the halls of Wilson Hospital were close and short, and Dad had gone out to pace in the damp September wind. He was praying, rounding the block for the fifth time, when the air quickened. He opened his eyes and discovered he was running—sprinting across the grass toward the door.

"How'd you know?" I adored this story, made him tell it all the time.

"God told me you were in trouble."

"Out loud? Did you hear Him?"

"Nope, not out loud. But He made me run, Reuben. I guess I figured it out on the way."

I had, in fact, been delivered some minutes before. My mother was dazed, propped against soggy pillows, unable to comprehend what Dr. Animas Nokes was telling her.

"He still isn't breathing, Mrs. Land."

"Give him to me!"

To this day I'm glad Dr. Nokes did not hand me over on demand. Tired as my mother was, who knows when she would've noticed? Instead he laid me down and rubbed me hard with a towel. He pounded my back; he rolled me over and massaged my chest. He breathed air into my mouth and nose—my chest rose, fell with a raspy whine, stayed fallen. Years later Dr. Nokes would tell my brother Davy that my delivery still disturbed his sleep. He'd never seen a child with such swampy lungs.

When Dad skidded into the room, Dr. Nokes was sitting on the side of the bed holding my mother's hand. She was wailing—I picture her as an old woman here, which is funny, since I was never to see her as one—and old Nokes was attempting to ease her grief. It was unavoidable, he was saying; nothing could be done; perhaps it was for the best.

I was lying uncovered on a metal table across the room.

Dad lifted me gently. I was very clean from all that rubbing, and I was gray and beginning to cool. A little clay boy is what I was.

"Breathe," Dad said.

I lay in his arms.

Dr. Nokes said, "Jeremiah, it has been twelve minutes."

"Breathe!" The picture I see is of Dad, brown hair short and wild, giving this order as if he expected nothing but obedience.

Dr. Nokes approached him. "Jeremiah. There would be brain damage now. His lungs can't fill."

Dad leaned down, laid me back on the table, took off his jacket and wrapped me in it—a black canvas jacket with a quilted lining, I have it still. He left my face uncovered.

"Sometimes," said Dr. Nokes, "there is something unworkable in one of the organs. A ventricle that won't pump correctly. A liver that poisons the blood." Dr. Nokes was a kindly and reasonable man. "Lungs that can't expand to take in air. In these cases," said Dr. Nokes, "we must trust in the Almighty to do what is best." At which Dad stepped across and smote Dr. Nokes with a right hand, so that the doctor went down and lay on his side with his pupils unfocused. As Mother cried out, Dad turned back to me, a clay child wrapped in a canvas coat, and said in a normal voice,

"Reuben Land, in the name of the living God I am telling you to breathe."

WEEK 7

Ask, Seek, Knock

OPENING PRAYER

Lord, hear my prayer when trouble glooms,
Let sorrow find a way,
And when the day of trouble comes,
Turn not thy face away.
—John Clare (English, 1793–1864)

SCRIPTURES

Psalm 86 | Ezra 9:5–15 | Hebrews 5:1–10 | Luke 11:9–13

READINGS

"Hymn to God My God, in My Sickness" by John Donne
"A Prayer That Will Be Answered" by Anna Kamieńska
"The Empty Cup" by Thomas Edward Brown
"Possible Answers to Prayer" by Scott Cairns
From "Psalm 86" by John Milton

PERSONAL PRAYER AND REFLECTION

CLOSING PRAYER

Quench my troubles,
For no one else can soothe them;
And let my eyes behold You,
For You are their light,
And I will keep them for You alone.
—John of the Cross (Spanish, 1542–1591)

READINGS FOR WEEK 7

Hymn to God My God, in My Sickness

JOHN DONNE (English, 1572–1631)

Since I am coming to that holy room,
Where, with thy choir of saints for evermore,
I shall be made thy music; as I come
I tune the instrument here at the door,
And what I must do then, think here before;

Whilst my physicians by their love are grown
Cosmographers, and I their map, who lie
Flat on this bed, that by them may be shown
That this is my south-west discovery,
Per fretum febris,[5] by these straits to die;

I joy, that in these straits I see my west;
For, though their currents yield return to none,
What shall my west hurt me? As west and east
In all flat maps (and I am one) are one,
So death doth touch the resurrection.

Is the Pacific Sea my home? Or are
The eastern riches? Is Jerusalem?
Anyan, and Magellan, and Gibraltar,
All straits, and none but straits, are ways to them,
Whether where Japhet dwelt, or Cham, or Shem.[66]

---

5 *Per fretum febris*—through the straits of fever.

6 *Japhet, Cham, or Shem*—the sons of Noah, believed by many in ancient and medieval times to be the fathers of the different human races, which settled in different parts of the world.

We think that Paradise and Calvary,
Christ's Cross, and Adam's tree, stood in one place;
Look Lord, and find both Adams met in me;
As the first Adam's sweat surrounds my face,
May the last Adam's blood my soul embrace.

So, in his purple wrapped receive me Lord;
By these his thorns, give me his other crown;
And as to others' souls I preached thy word,
Be this my text, my sermon to mine own,
Therefore that he may raise, the Lord throws down.

A Prayer That Will Be Answered

ANNA KAMIEŃSKA (Polish, 1920–1986)

Lord let me suffer a lot
and then let me die

Allow me to walk through silence
Let nothing not even fear linger after me

Make the world go on as it always has
let the sea continue to kiss the shore

Let grass still remain green
so a little frog could find shelter in it

and someone could bury his face
and weep his heart out

Make a day dawn so bright
it seems there is no more suffering

And let my poem be transparent as a windowpane
against which a straying bee hits its head

The Empty Cup

THOMAS EDWARD BROWN (British, 1830–1897)

Fly away, bark,
  Over the sea!
Take thou my grief,
  Take it with thee!
Bear it afar
  Unto the shore
Where the old griefs are
  For evermore!
O, it was hard!
  Take it away—
Pressed on my heart
  By night and by day.
I will not have it;
  Let it go, let it go!
Shall I have nothing
  But wailing and woe?

Let it be, let it be!
  O, bring it again!
Bring my sorrow to me,
  Bring weeping and pain!
Bring my sorrow to me—
  After all, it is mine
O God of my heart,
  I will not repine.
For I feel such a lack,
  And I am such a stone—
Bring it back, bring it back!
  It is better to groan
With my old, old load

Than to search within,
And find nothing there
But folly and sin.
O, I cannot bear
This empty cup:
If it must be with gall,
Fill it up! fill it up!
Fill my soul, fill my soul!
And I will bless
The hand that filleth
Mine emptiness.

Possible Answers to Prayer
SCOTT CAIRNS (American, contemporary)

Your petitions—though they continue to bear
just the one signature—have been duly recorded.
Your anxieties—despite their constant,

relatively narrow scope and inadvertent
entertainment value—nonetheless serve
to bring your person vividly to mind.

Your repentance—all but obscured beneath
a burgeoning, yellow fog of frankly more
conspicuous resentment—is sufficient.

Your intermittent concern for the sick,
the suffering, the needy poor is sometimes
recognizable to me, if not to them.

Your angers, your zeal, your lipsmackingly
righteous indignation toward the many
whose habits and sympathies offend you—

these must burn away before you'll apprehend
how near I am, with what fervor I adore
precisely these, the several who rouse your passion.

From *"Psalm 86"*

John Milton (English, 1608–1674)

Thy gracious ear, O Lord, incline,
   O hear me I thee pray,
For I am poor, and almost pine
   With need, and sad decay.
Preserve my soul, for I have trod
   Thy ways, and love the just;
Save thou thy servant O my God
   Who still in thee doth trust.
Pity me Lord for daily thee
   I call; O make rejoice
Thy servant's soul; for Lord to thee
   I lift my soul and voice;
For thou art good, thou Lord art prone
   To pardon, thou to all
Art full of mercy, thou alone
   To them that on thee call.
Unto my supplication Lord
   Give ear, and to the cry
Of my incessant prayers afford
   Thy hearing graciously.

I in the day of my distress
  Will call on thee for aid;
For thou wilt grant me free access
  And answer, what I prayed.
Like thee among the gods is none
  O Lord, nor any works
Of all that other gods have done
  Like to thy glorious works.
The nations all whom thou hast made
  Shall come, and all shall frame
To bow them low before thee Lord,
  And glorify thy name.
For great thou art, and wonders great
  By thy strong hand are done;
Thou in thy everlasting seat
  Remainest God alone. . . .
. . . Teach me O Lord thy way most right;
  I in thy truth will bide;
To fear thy name my heart unite,
  So shall it never slide.
Thee will I praise O Lord my God
  Thee honor, and adore
With my whole heart, and blaze abroad
  Thy name for evermore.
For great thy mercy is toward me,
  And thou hast freed my soul,
Ev'n from the lowest Hell set free,
  From deepest darkness foul.
O God the proud against me rise
  And violent men are met
To seek my life, and in their eyes
  No fear of thee have set.

But thou Lord art the God most mild,
  Readiest thy grace to show,
Slow to be angry, and art styled
  Most merciful, most true.
O turn to me thy face at length,
  And me have mercy on;
Unto thy servant give thy strength,
  And save thy handmaid's son.
Some sign of good to me afford,
  And let my foes then see
And be ashamed, because thou Lord
  Dost help and comfort me.

WEEK 8

Quarrels with Heaven

OPENING PRAYER

O God, why has thou thus
Repulsed, and scattered us?
Shall now thy wrath no limits hold,
But ever smoke and burn
Till it to ashes turn
The chosen folk of thy dear fold?
—Mary Herbert (English, 1561–1621)

SCRIPTURES

Psalm 10 | Job 40:1–14 | Romans 2:1–11 | Matthew 20:1–16

READINGS

"Speak" by Harold J. Recinos
"The Collar" by George Herbert
From "Song of the Soul and the Bridegroom" by John of the Cross
From *The Death of Ivan Ilyich* by Leo Tolstoy

PERSONAL PRAYER AND REFLECTION

CLOSING PRAYER

Reveal Your presence,
And let the vision and Your beauty kill me,
Behold the malady
Of love is incurable
Except in Your presence and before Your face.
—John of the Cross (Spanish, 1542–1591)

READINGS FOR WEEK 8

Speak

HAROLD J. RECINOS (Puerto Rican/Guatemalan-American, contemporary)

I sit and hear
about the man
from Guatemala

shot last week
by cops who never
sob about wrong

doing. I see
bony children in
unlit apartments

neglected, abused,
desperately crying
in beaten mothers'

arms. I hear people
talk about martyrs, agony
without end, the death

of the world, the vain
cries everywhere, the
churches unable to see

and hear beyond their
sullen Sabbath. I
dwell on the silence

of God.

The Collar

George Herbert (English, 1593–1633)

I struck the board, and cried, No more.
I will abroad.
What? shall I ever sigh and pine?
My lines and life are free; free as the road,
Loose as the wind, as large as store.
Shall I be still in suit?
Have I no harvest but a thorn
To let me blood, and not restore
What I have lost with cordial fruit?
Sure there was wine
Before my sighs did dry it: there was corn
Before my tears did drown it.
Is the year only lost to me?
Have I no bays to crown it?
No flowers, no garlands gay? all blasted?
All wasted?
Not so, my heart: but there is fruit,
And thou hast hands.
Recover all thy sigh-blown age
On double pleasures: leave thy cold dispute
Of what is fit, and not. Forsake thy cage,

Thy rope of sands,
Which petty thoughts have made, and made to thee
Good cable, to enforce and draw,
And be thy law,
While thou didst wink and wouldst not see.
Away; take heed:
I will abroad.
Call in thy death's head there: tie up thy fears.
He that forbears
To suit and serve his need,
Deserves his load.
But as I raved and grew more fierce and wild,
At every word,
Me thought I heard one calling, *Child:*
And I replied, *My Lord.*

FROM *"Song of the Soul and the Bridegroom"*

JOHN OF THE CROSS (Spanish, 1542–1591)

Oh! who can heal me?
Give me at once Yourself,
Send me no more
A messenger
Who cannot tell me what I wish.

All they who serve are telling me
Of Your unnumbered graces;
And all wound me more and more,
And something leaves me dying,
I know not what, of which they are darkly speaking.

But how you persevere, O life,
Not living where you live;
The arrows bring death
Which you receive
From your conceptions of the Beloved.

Why, after wounding
This heart, have You not healed it?
And why, after stealing it,
Have You thus abandoned it,
And not carried away the stolen prey?

FROM *The Death of Ivan Ilyich*

LEO TOLSTOY (Russian, 1828–1910)

[Editor's note: Ivan Ilyich thought he had led a "good" life, that is, successful in his law profession and upwardly mobile in society. But when he falls ill and realizes he is dying, his careful world begins to unravel. Unwilling to face the truth, he rejects the help of his good servant Gerasim and then finds himself in a kind of Socratic argument with another voice.]

Till about three in the morning he was in a state of stupefied misery. It seemed to him that he and his pain were being thrust into a narrow, deep black sack, but though they were pushed further and further in they could not be pushed to the bottom. And this, terrible enough in itself, was accompanied by suffering. He was frightened yet wanted to fall through the sack, he struggled but yet cooperated. And suddenly he broke through, fell, and regained consciousness. Gerasim was sitting at the foot of the bed dozing quietly and patiently, while he himself lay with his emaciated stockinged legs resting on Gerasim's shoulders; the same shaded candle was there and the same unceasing pain.

"Go away, Gerasim," he whispered.

"It's all right, sir. I'll stay a while."

"No. Go away."

He removed his legs from Gerasim's shoulders, turned sideways onto his arm, and felt sorry for himself. He only waited till Gerasim had gone into the next room and then restrained himself no longer but wept like a child. He wept on account of his helplessness, his terrible loneliness, the cruelty of man, the cruelty of God, and the absence of God.

"Why hast Thou done all this? Why hast Thou brought me here? Why, why dost Thou torment me so terribly?"

He did not expect an answer and yet wept because there was no answer and could be none. The pain again grew more acute, but he did not stir and did not call. He said to himself: "Go on! Strike me! But what is it for? What have I done to Thee? What is it for?"

Then he grew quiet and not only ceased weeping but even held his breath and became all attention. It was as though he were listening not to an audible voice but to the voice of his soul, to the current of thoughts arising within him.

"What is it you want?" was the first clear conception capable of expression in words, that he heard. . . .

[continued below]

FROM *The Death of Ivan Ilyich*

"What do you want? What do you want?" he repeated to himself.

"What do I want? To live and not to suffer," he answered.

And again he listened with such concentrated attention that even his pain did not distract him.

"To live? How?" asked his inner voice.

"Why, to live as I used to—well and pleasantly."

"As you lived before, well and pleasantly?" the voice repeated.

And in imagination he began to recall the best moments of his pleasant life. But strange to say none of those best moments of his pleasant life now seemed at all what they had then seemed—none of them except the first recollections of childhood. There, in childhood, there had been something really pleasant with which it would be possible to live if it could return. But the child who had experienced that happiness existed no longer; it was like a reminiscence of somebody else.

As soon as the period began which had produced the present Ivan Ilyich, all that had then seemed joys now melted before his sight and turned into something trivial and often nasty.

And the further he departed from childhood and the nearer he came to the present the more worthless and doubtful were the joys. This began with the School of Law. A little that was really good was still found there—there was light-heartedness, friendship, and hope. But in the upper classes there had already been fewer of such good moments. Then during the first years of his official career, when he was in the service of the governor, some pleasant moments again occurred: they were the memories of love for a woman. Then all became confused and there was still less of what was good; later on again there was still less that was good, and the further he went the less there was. His marriage, a mere accident, then the disenchantment that followed it, his wife's bad breath and the sensuality and hypocrisy: then that deadly official life and those preoccupations about money, a year of it, and two, and ten, and twenty, and always the same thing. And the longer it lasted the more deadly it became. "It is as if I had been going downhill while I imagined I was going up. And that is really what it was. I was going up in public opinion, but to the same extent life was ebbing away from me. And now it is all done and there is only death.

"Then what does it mean? Why? It can't be that life is so senseless and horrible. But if it really has been so horrible and senseless, why must I die and die in agony? There is something wrong!

"Maybe I did not live as I ought to have done," it suddenly occurred to him. "But how could that be, when I did everything properly?" he replied, and immediately dismissed from his mind this, the sole solution of all the riddles of life and death, as something quite impossible.

"Then what do you want now? To live? Live how? Live as you lived in the law courts when the usher proclaimed 'The judge is coming!' The judge is coming, the judge!" he repeated to himself. "Here he is, the judge. But I am not guilty!" he exclaimed angrily. "What is it for?" And he ceased crying, but turning his face to the wall continued to ponder on the same question: Why, and for what purpose, is there all this horror? But however much he pondered he found no answer. And whenever the thought occurred to him, as it often did, that it all resulted from his not having lived as he ought to have done, he at once recalled the correctness of his whole life and dismissed so strange an idea.

WEEK 9

Dark Night

OPENING PRAYER

O eternal and most gracious God, even though you created darkness before light in Creation, you so multiplied that light that it illuminated the day and the night. Though you have permitted some clouds of sadness to darken my soul, I humbly bless and glorify your holy name, for you have permitted me the light of the Spirit, against which the prince of darkness cannot prevail nor hinder the illumination of our darkest nights or saddest thoughts.

—JOHN DONNE (English, 1572–1631)

SCRIPTURES

PSALM 88 | ESTHER 4:1–17 | 2 CORINTHIANS 4:7–18 | MARK 14:32–42

READINGS

"The Companionable Dark" by KATHLEEN NORRIS
"I wake and feel the fell of dark, not day" by GERARD MANLEY HOPKINS
"What if this present were the world's last night?"
(Holy Sonnets: XIII) by JOHN DONNE
From *Diary of an Old Soul* by GEORGE MACDONALD
From *Jacob Have I Loved* by KATHERINE PATERSON

PERSONAL PRAYER AND REFLECTION

CLOSING PRAYER

And now 'tis night, and night within,
O God, the light hath fled!

I have not kept the vow I made
When morn its glories shed.
—adapted from the poetry of GREGORY OF NAZIANZUS (Cappadocia/modern-day Turkey, AD 325–390)

READINGS FOR WEEK 9

The Companionable Dark

KATHLEEN NORRIS (American, contemporary)

of here and now,
seed lying dormant
in the earth. The dark
to which all lost things come—scarves
and rings and precious photographs, and
of course, our beloved
dead. The brooding dark,
our most vulnerable hours, limbs loose
in sleep, mouths agape.
The faithful dark,
where each door leads,
each one of us, alone.
The dark of God come close
as breath, our one companion
all the way through, the dark
of a needle's eye.

Not the easy dark
of dusk and candles,
but dark from which comforts flee.

The deep down dark
of one by one,
dark of wind
and dust, dark in which stars burn.
The floodwater dark
of hope, Jesus in agony
in the garden, Esther pacing
her bitter palace. A dark
by which we see, dark like truth,
like flesh on bone:
Help me, who am alone,
and have no help but thee.

I wake and feel the fell of dark, not day

GERARD MANLEY HOPKINS (English, 1844–1889)

I wake and feel the fell of dark, not day.
What hours, O what black hours we have spent
This night! what sights you, heart, saw, ways you went!
And more must, in yet longer light's delay.

With witness I speak this. But where I say
Hours I mean years, mean life. And my lament
Is cries countless, cries like dead letters sent
To dearest him that lives alas! away.

I am gall, I am heartburn. God's most deep decree
Bitter would have me taste: my taste was me;
Bones built in me, flesh filled, blood brimmed the curse.

Selfyeast of spirit a dull dough sours. I see
The lost are like this, and their scourge to be
As I am mine, their sweating selves; but worse.

What if this present were the world's last night? (Holy Sonnets: XIII)

JOHN DONNE (English, 1572–1631)

What if this present were the world's last night?
Mark in my heart, O soul, where thou dost dwell,
The picture of Christ crucified, and tell
Whether that countenance can thee affright,
Tears in his eyes quench the amazing light,
Blood fills his frowns, which from his pierced head fell,
And can that tongue adjudge thee unto hell,
Which prayed forgiveness for his foes' fierce spite?
No, no; but as in my idolatry
I said to all my profane mistresses,
Beauty, of pity, foulness only is
A sign of rigor: so I say to thee,
To wicked spirits are horrid shapes assigned,
This beauteous form assures a piteous mind.

FROM *Diary of an Old Soul*

GEORGE MACDONALD (Scottish, 1824–1905)

Sometimes, hard-trying, it seems I cannot pray—
For doubt, and pain, and anger, and all strife,
Yet some poor half-fledged prayer-bird from the nest
May fall, flit, fly, perch—crouch in the bowery breast
Of the large, nation-healing tree of life;
Moveless there sit through all the burning day,
And on my heart at night a fresh leaf cooling lay.

FROM *Jacob Have I Loved*

KATHERINE PATERSON (American, contemporary)

[Editor's note: Paterson's Newbery-winning novella tells the story of twin sisters growing up on the Chesapeake Bay. The oldest twin, Louise—plain, strong, often overlooked—struggles to love her beautiful, attention-getting sister, Caroline. Here she lies awake at night after a particularly defeating episode with Caroline, unable to pray without feeling angry and vengeful.]

That night I lay in bed with an emptiness chewing away inside of me. I said my prayers, trying to push it away with ritual, but it kept oozing back round the worn edges of the words. I had deliberately given up "Now I lay me down to sleep" two years before as being too babyish a prayer and had been using since then the Lord's Prayer attached to a number of formula "God blesses." But that night "Now I lay me" came back unbidden in the darkness.

Now I lay me down to sleep,
I pray the Lord my soul to keep.
If I should die before I wake,
I pray the Lord my soul to take.

"If I should die . . ." It didn't push back the emptiness. It snatched and tore at it, making the hole larger and darker. "If I should die . . ." I tried to shake the words away with "Yea, though I walk through the valley of the shadow of death, I shall fear no evil, for behold, thou art with me . . ."

There was something about the thought of God being with me that made me feel more alone than ever. It was like being with Caroline.

She was so sure, so present, so easy, so light and gold, while I was all gray and shadow. I was not ugly or monstrous. That might have been better. Monsters always command attention, if only for their freakishness. My parents would have wrung their hands and tried to make it up to me, as parents will with a handicapped or especially ugly child. Even Call, his nose too large for his small face, had a certain satisfactory ugliness. And his mother and grandmother did their share of worrying about him. But I had never caused my parents "a minute's worry." Didn't they know that worry proves you care? Didn't they realize that I needed their worry to assure myself that I was worth something?

I worried about them. I feared for my father's safety every time there was a storm on the Bay, and for my mother's whenever she took the ferry to the mainland. I read magazine articles in the school library on health and gave them mental physical examinations and tested the health of their marriage. "Can this marriage succeed?" Probably not. They had nothing in common as far as I could tell from the questionnaires I read. I even worried about Caroline, though why should I bother when everyone else spent their lives fretting over her?

I longed for the day when they would have to notice me, give me all the attention and concern that was my due. In my wildest daydreams there was a scene taken from the dreams of Joseph. Joseph dreamed that one day all his brothers and his parents as well would bow down to him. I tried to imagine Caroline bowing down to me. At first, of course, she laughingly refused, but then a giant hand descended from the sky and shoved her to her knees. Her face grew dark. "Oh, Wheeze," she began to apologize. "Call me no longer Wheeze, but Sara Louise," I said grandly, smiling in the darkness, casting off the nickname she had diminished me with since we were two.

WEEK 10

A Haunted Conscience

OPENING PRAYER

Take from my head the thorn-wreath brown!
No mortal grief deserves that crown.
O supreme Love, chief misery,
The sharp regalia are for Thee
Whose days eternally go on!
—Elizabeth Barrett Browning
(English, 1806–1861)

SCRIPTURES

Psalm 38 | 2 Samuel 12:1–14 | Romans 7:14–25 | Luke 16:19–31

READINGS

"Sin (I)" by George Herbert
"Hester Prynne Recalls a Sunday in June" by Kathleen Norris
"Lines Written Under the Influence" by William Cowper
"Who Shall Deliver Me?" by Christina Rossetti
From *The Scarlet Letter* by Nathaniel Hawthorne

PERSONAL PRAYER AND REFLECTION

CLOSING PRAYER

O Christ, have pity on all men when they come
Unto the border haunted of dismay;
When that they know not draweth very near—
The other thing, the opposite of day,
Formless and ghastly, sick, and gaping-dumb,

Before which even love does lose his cheer,
O radiant Christ, remember then thy fear.
—George MacDonald (Scottish, 1824–1905)

READINGS FOR WEEK 10

Sin (I)

George Herbert (English, 1593–1633)

Lord, with what care hast thou begirt us round!
  Parents first season us: then schoolmasters
  Deliver us to laws; they send us bound
To rules of reason, holy messengers,
Pulpits and Sundays, sorrow dogging sin,
  Afflictions sorted, anguish of all sizes,
  Fine nets and stratagems to catch us in,
Bibles laid open, millions of surprises,
Blessings beforehand, ties of gratefulness,
  The sound of glory ringing in our ears:
  Without, our shame; within our consciences;
Angels and grace, eternal hopes and fears.
  Yet all these fences and their whole array
  One cunning bosom-sin blows quite away.

Hester Prynne Recalls a Sunday in June

KATHLEEN NORRIS (American, contemporary)

Our affair had begun,
a sweet time.
I looked forward so to seeing him,
dark figure in sunlight.
When the moment struck—his sermon
drew fire—I saw quite clearly
that he had ritual,
law, the Word,
and I had nothing but myself.

All that
is in the past.
Now respectable women
seek my hand; I must find each broken thread
and make it sing.

They stay and talk now
as I sew. It's as if they expect me
to tell them something,
a secret I brought up
out of chaos.

But I've been too long outside
the comfort they found
in other kingdoms. Pray for me,
I tell them,
if you are my friends.

———

Lines Written Under the Influence

WILLIAM COWPER (English, 1731–1800)

Hatred and vengeance,—my eternal portion
Scarce can endure delay of execution,—
Wait with impatient readiness to seize my
Soul in a moment.

Damned below Judas; more abhorred than he was,
Who for a few pence sold his holy Master!
Twice betrayed, Jesus me, the last delinquent,
Deems the profanest.

Man disavows, and Deity disowns me,
Hell might afford my miseries a shelter;
Therefore, Hell keeps her ever-hungry mouths all
Bolted against me.

Hard lot! encompassed with a thousand dangers;
Weary, faint, trembling with a thousand terrors,
I'm called, if vanquished, to receive a sentence
Worse than Abiram's.[7]

Him the vindictive rod of angry Justice
Sent quick and howling to the center headlong;
I fed with judgment, in a fleshy tomb, am
Buried above ground.

———

7 Abiram—see Numbers 16.

Who Shall Deliver Me?

Christina Rossetti (English, 1830–1894)

God strengthen me to bear myself;
That heaviest weight of all to bear,
Inalienable weight of care.

All others are outside myself;
I lock my door and bar them out,
The turmoil, tedium, gad-about.

I lock my door upon myself,
And bar them out; but who shall wall
Self from myself, most loathed of all?

If I could once lay down myself,
And start self-purged upon the race
That all must run! Death runs apace.

If I could set aside myself,
And start with lightened heart upon
The road by all men overgone!

God harden me against myself,
This coward with pathetic voice
Who craves for ease, and rest, and joys:

Myself, arch-traitor to myself;
My hollowest friend, my deadliest foe,
My clog whatever road I go.

Yet One there is can curb myself,
Can roll the strangling load from me,
Break off the yoke and set me free.

———

FROM *The Scarlet Letter*

NATHANIEL HAWTHORNE (American, 1804-1864)

[Editor's note: Many assume that *The Scarlet Letter* is about the harsh judgment that a Puritan society can place on an ordinary sinner like Hester Prynne, who is forced to wear a red *A* for "adultery" after she is found to be with child in her husband's long absence. But no judgment is greater than the private, haunting agony of her lover, Reverend Dimmesdale, who cannot bring himself to publicly admit his sin and yet cannot bear the burden of his secret. Here his inner battle reaches fever pitch.]

On one of those ugly nights, which we have faintly hinted at, but forborne to picture forth, the minister started from his chair. A new thought had struck him. There might be a moment's peace in it. Attiring himself with as much care as if it had been for public worship, and precisely in the same manner, he stole softly down the staircase, undid the door, and issued forth.

Walking in the shadow of a dream, as it were, and perhaps actually under the influence of a species of somnambulism, Mr. Dimmesdale reached the spot, where, now so long since, Hester Prynne had lived through her first hours of public ignominy. The same platform or scaffold, black and weather-stained with the storm or sunshine of seven long years, and footworn, too, with the tread of many culprits who had since ascended it, remained standing beneath the balcony of the meeting-house. The minister went up the steps.

It was an obscure night of early May. An unvaried pall of cloud muffled the whole expanse of sky from zenith to horizon. If the same multitude which had stood as eye-witnesses while Hester Prynne sustained her punishment could now have been summoned forth, they would have discerned no face above the platform, nor hardly the outline of a human shape, in the dark grey of the midnight. But the town was all asleep. There was no peril of discovery. The minister might stand there, if it so pleased him, until morning should redden in the east, without other risk than that the dank and chill night-air would creep into his frame, and stiffen his joints with rheumatism, and clog his throat with catarrh and cough; thereby defrauding the expectant audience of tomorrow's prayer and sermon. No eye could see him, save that ever-wakeful one which had seen him in his closet, wielding the bloody scourge. Why, then, had he come thither? Was it but the mockery of penitence? A mockery, indeed, but in which his soul trifled with itself! A mockery at which angels blushed and wept, while fiends rejoiced, with jeering laughter! He had been driven hither by the impulse of that Remorse which dogged him everywhere, and whose own sister and closely linked companion was that Cowardice which invariably drew him back, with her tremulous grip, just when the other impulse had hurried him to the verge of a disclosure. Poor, miserable man! what right did infirmity like his to burden itself with crime? Crime is for the iron-nerved, who have their choice either to endure it, or, if it press too hard, to exert their fierce and savage strength for a good purpose, and fling it off at once! This feeble and most sensitive of spirits could do neither, yet continually did one thing or another, which intertwined, in the same inextricable knot, the agony of heaven-defying guilt and vain repentance.

[continued below]

FROM *The Scarlet Letter*

And thus, while standing on the scaffold, in this vain show of expiation, Mr. Dimmesdale was overcome with a great horror of mind, as if the universe were gazing at a scarlet token on his naked breast, right over his heart. On that spot, in very truth, there was, and there had long been, the gnawing and poisonous tooth of bodily pain. Without any effort of his will, or power to restrain himself, he shrieked aloud; an outcry that went pealing through the night, and was beaten back from one house to another, and reverberated from the hills in the background; as if a company of devils, detecting so much misery and terror in it, had made a plaything of the sound, and were bandying it to and fro.

"It is done!" muttered the minister, covering his face with his hands. "The whole town will awake, and hurry forth, and find me here!"

But it was not so. The shriek had perhaps sounded with a far greater power, to his own startled ears, than it actually possessed. The town did not awake; or, if it did, the drowsy slumberers mistook the cry either for something frightful in a dream, or for the noise of witches; whose voices, at that period, were often heard to pass over the settlements or lonely cottages, as they rode with Satan through the air. The clergyman, therefore, hearing no symptoms of disturbance, uncovered his eyes and looked about him.

WEEK 11

Unexpected Encounter

OPENING PRAYER

O Lord in me there lieth nought
  But to thy search revealèd lies:
    For when I sit
    Thou markest it;
  No less thou notest when I rise
Yea, closest closet of my thought
  Hath open windows to thine eyes.
—MARY HERBERT (English, 1561–1621)

SCRIPTURES

PSALM 36 | JONAH 1:1–16 | ACTS 9:1–9 | JOHN 4:7–26

READINGS

From "Psalm 139" by MARY HERBERT
From "The Hound of Heaven" by FRANCIS THOMPSON
From "The Queer Feet" in *The Innocence of Father Brown* by G. K. CHESTERTON

PERSONAL PRAYER AND REFLECTION

CLOSING PRAYER

If making makes us Thine then Thine we are,
  And if redemption we are twice Thine own:
If once Thou didst come down from heaven afar
  To seek us and to find us, how not save?

Comfort us, save us, leave us not alone,
Thou Who didst die our death and fill our grave.
—CHRISTINA ROSSETTI (English, 1830–1894)

READINGS FOR WEEK 11

FROM *"Psalm 139"*

MARY HERBERT (English, 1561–1621)

Thou walkest with me when I walk;
When to my bed for rest I go,
I find thee there,
And everywhere;
Not youngest thought in me doth grow,
No, not one word I cast to talk,
But yet unuttered thou dost know.

If forth I march, thou goest before,
If back I turn, thou com'st behind;
So forth nor back
Thy guard I lack,
Nay on me too thy hand I find.
Well I thy wisdom may adore,
But never reach with earthy mind. . . .

. . . O Sun, whom light nor flight can match,
Suppose thy lightful, flightful wings,
Thou lend to me,
And I could flee
As far as thee the evening brings,
Ev'n to West he would me catch
Nor should I lurk with western things.

———

FROM *"The Hound of Heaven"*

FRANCIS THOMPSON (English, 1859–1907)

I fled Him, down the nights and down the days;
I fled Him, down the arches of the years;
I fled Him, down the labyrinthine ways
Of my own mind; and in the mist of tears
I hid from Him, and under running laughter.
Up vistaed hopes I sped;
And shot, precipitated,
Adown Titanic glooms of chasmèd fears,
From those strong Feet that followed, followed after.
But with unhurrying chase,
And unperturbèd pace,
Deliberate speed, majestic instancy,
They beat—and a Voice beat
More instant than the Feet—
"All things betray thee, who betrayest Me." . . .

. . . Now of that long pursuit
Comes on at hand the bruit;
That Voice is round me like a bursting sea:
"And is thy earth so marred,
Shattered in shard on shard?
Lo, all things fly thee, for thou fliest Me!
Strange, piteous, futile thing!
Wherefore should any set thee love apart?
Seeing none but I makes much of naught" (He said),
"And human love needs human meriting:
How hast thou merited—
Of all man's clotted clay the dingiest clot?
Alack, thou knowest not
How little worthy of any love thou art!

Whom wilt thou find to love ignoble thee,
 Save Me, save only Me?
All which I took from thee I did but take,
 Not for thy harms,
But just that thou might'st seek it in My arms.
 All which thy child's mistake
Fancies as lost, I have stored for thee at home:
 Rise, clasp My hand, and come!"
 Halts by me that footfall:
 Is my gloom, after all,
Shade of His hand, outstretched caressingly?
 "Ah, fondest, blindest, weakest,
 I am He Whom thou seekest!
Thou dravest[8] love from thee, who dravest Me."

FROM "The Queer Feet" in *The Innocence of Father Brown*
G. K. CHESTERTON (English, 1874–1936)

[Editor's note: The annual club dinner of "The Twelve True Fishermen," held at the exclusive Vernon Hotel, is interrupted when the club's pearl-studded silverware disappears. It is the unassuming Father Brown who comes to their rescue after hearing a pattern of footsteps near the cloak room which excites his curiosity. The culprit turns out to be an internationally famous burglar whom he had encountered in a previous episode but failed to catch. Here Brown surprises the culprit by confronting him not only with his crime but also with the truth of his spiritual condition.]

8 *dravest*—archaic usage for "drove" or "chased."

Father Brown flung down his paper, and, knowing the office door to be locked, went at once into the cloak room on the other side. The attendant of this place was temporarily absent, probably because the only guests were at dinner and his office was a sinecure. After groping through a grey forest of overcoats, he found that the dim cloak room opened on the lighted corridor in the form of a sort of counter or half-door, like most of the counters across which we have all handed umbrellas and received tickets. There was a light immediately above the semicircular arch of this opening. It threw little illumination on Father Brown himself, who seemed a mere dark outline against the dim sunset window behind him. But it threw an almost theatrical light on the man who stood outside the cloak room in the corridor.

He was an elegant man in very plain evening dress; tall, but with an air of not taking up much room; one felt that he could have slid along like a shadow where many smaller men would have been obvious and obstructive. His face, now flung back in the lamplight, was swarthy and vivacious, the face of a foreigner. His figure was good, his manners good humored and confident; a critic could only say that his black coat was a shade below his figure and manners, and even bulged and bagged in an odd way. The moment he caught sight of Brown's black silhouette against the sunset, he tossed down a scrap of paper with a number and called out with amiable authority: "I want my hat and coat, please; I find I have to go away at once."

Father Brown took the paper without a word, and obediently went to look for the coat; it was not the first menial work he had done in his life. He brought it and laid it on the counter; meanwhile, the strange gentleman who had been feeling in his waistcoat pocket, said laughing: "I haven't got any silver; you can keep this." And he threw down half a sovereign, and caught up his coat.

Father Brown's figure remained quite dark and still; but in that instant he had lost his head. His head was always most valuable when he had lost it. In such moments he put two and two together and made four million. Often the Catholic Church (which is wedded to common sense) did not approve of it. Often he did not approve of it himself. But it was real inspiration—important at rare crises—when whosoever shall lose his head the same shall save it.

"I think, sir," he said civilly, "that you have some silver in your pocket."

The tall gentleman stared. "Hang it," he cried, "if I choose to give you gold, why should you complain?"

"Because silver is sometimes more valuable than gold," said the priest mildly; "that is, in large quantities."

The stranger looked at him curiously. Then he looked still more curiously up the passage towards the main entrance. Then he looked back at Brown again, and then he looked very carefully at the window beyond Brown's head, still colored with the after-glow of the storm. Then he seemed to make up his mind. He put one hand on the counter, vaulted over as easily as an acrobat and towered above the priest, putting one tremendous hand upon his collar.

"Stand still," he said, in a hacking whisper. "I don't want to threaten you, but—"

"I do want to threaten you," said Father Brown in a voice like a rolling drum, "I want to threaten you with the worm that dieth not, and the fire that is not quenched."

"You're a rum sort of cloak-room clerk," said the other.

"I am a priest, Monsieur Flambeau," said Brown, "and I am ready to hear your confession."

The other stood gasping for a few moments, and then staggered back into a chair.

[continued below]

FROM *"The Queer Feet"*

"Hallo, there!" called out the duke [to Father Brown]. "Have you seen anyone pass?"

The short figure did not answer the question directly, but merely said: "Perhaps I have got what you are looking for, gentlemen."

They paused, wavering and wondering, while he quietly went to the back of the cloak room, and came back with both hands full of shining silver, which he laid out on the counter as calmly as a salesman. It took the form of a dozen quaintly shaped forks and knives.

"You—you—" began the colonel, quite thrown off his balance at last. Then he peered into the dim little room and saw two things: first, that the short, black-clad man was dressed like a clergyman; and second, that the window of the room behind him was burst, as if someone had passed violently through.

"Valuable things to deposit in a cloak room, aren't they?" remarked the clergyman, with cheerful composure.

"Did—did you steal those things?" stammered Mr. Audley, with staring eyes.

"If I did," said the cleric pleasantly, "at least I am bringing them back again."

"But you didn't," said Colonel Pound, still staring at the broken window.

"To make a clean breast of it, I didn't," said the other, with some humor. And he seated himself quite gravely on a stool.

"But you know who did," said the colonel.

"I don't know his real name," said the priest placidly, "but I know something of his fighting weight, and a great deal about his spiritual difficulties. I formed the physical estimate when he was trying to throttle me, and the moral estimate when he repented."

"Oh, I say—repented!" cried young Chester, with a sort of crow of laughter.

Father Brown got to his feet, putting his hands behind him. "Odd, isn't it," he said, "that a thief and a vagabond should repent, when so many who are rich and secure remain hard and frivolous, and without fruit for God or man? But there, if you will excuse me, you trespass a little upon my province. If you doubt the penitence as a practical fact, there are your knives and forks. You are The Twelve True Fishers, and there are all your silver fish. But He has made me a fisher of men."

"Did you catch this man?" asked the colonel, frowning.

Father Brown looked him full in his frowning face. "Yes," he said, "I caught him, with an unseen hook and an invisible line which is long enough to let him wander to the ends of the world, and still to bring him back with a twitch upon the thread."

WEEK 12

Cry from the Depths

OPENING PRAYER

Lord, I would have me love thee from the deeps—
Of troubled thought, of pain, of weariness.
Through seething wastes below, billows above,
My soul should rise in eager, hungering leaps;
Through thorny thicks, through sands unstable press—
Out of my dream to him who slumbers not nor sleeps.
—GEORGE MACDONALD (Scottish, 1824–1905)

SCRIPTURES

PSALM 69 | JONAH 2:1–9 | ACTS 27:13–26 | MATTHEW 14:22–33

READINGS

"Out of the deep" by CHRISTINA ROSSETTI
"The Ribs and Terrors . . ." by HERMAN MELVILLE
"Discontent" by ELIZABETH BARRETT BROWNING
"A Hymn to Christ . . ." by JOHN DONNE
From *Moby Dick* by HERMAN MELVILLE

PERSONAL PRAYER AND REFLECTION

CLOSING PRAYER

From depth of sin and from a deep despair,
From depth of death, from depth of heart's sorrow,
From this deep cave of darkness' deep repair,

Thee have I called, O Lord, to be my borow.[9]
  Thou in my voice, O Lord, perceive and hear
  My heart, my hope, my plaint, my overthrow.
—Sir Thomas Wyatt (English, 1503–1542)

READINGS FOR WEEK 12

Out of the deep

CHRISTINA ROSSETTI (English, 1830–1894)

Have mercy, Thou my God; mercy, my God;
  For I can hardly bear life day by day:
  Be here or there I fret myself away:
Lo for Thy staff I have but felt Thy rod
Along this tedious desert path long trod.
  When will Thy judgment judge me, Yea or Nay?
  I pray for grace; but then my sins unpray
My prayer: on holy ground I fool stand shod.
While still Thou haunts't me, faint upon the cross,
  A sorrow beyond sorrow in Thy look,
Unutterable craving for my soul.
All faithful Thou, Lord: I, not Thou, forsook
  Myself; I traitor slunk back from the goal:
Lord, I repent; help Thou my helpless loss.

———

9 *borow*—shelter.

The Ribs and Terrors . . .

HERMAN MELVILLE (American, 1819–1891)

The ribs and terrors in the whale,
 Arched over me a dismal gloom,
While all God's sun-lit waves rolled by,
 And lift me to a deeper doom.

I saw the opening maw of hell,
 With endless pains and sorrows there;
Which none but they that feel can tell—
 Oh, I was plunging to despair.

In black distress, I called my God,
 When I could scarce believe Him mine,
He bowed His ear to my complaints—
 No more the whale did me confine.

With speed He flew to my relief,
 As on a radiant dolphin borne;
Awful, yet bright, as lightning shone
 The face of my Deliverer God.

My song for ever shall record
 That terrible, that joyful hour;
I give the glory to my God,
 His all the mercy and the power.

———

Discontent

ELIZABETH BARRETT BROWNING (English, 1806–1861)

Light human nature is too lightly tossed
And ruffled without cause, complaining on—
Restless with rest, until, being overthrown,
It learneth to lie quiet. Let a frost
Or a small wasp have crept to the inner-most
Of our ripe peach, or let the willful sun
Shine westward of our window,—straight we run
A furlong's sigh as if the world were lost.
But what time through the heart and through the brain
God hath transfixed us,—we, so moved before,
Attain to a calm. Ay, shouldering weights of pain,
We anchor in deep waters, safe from shore,
And hear submissive o'er the stormy main
God's chartered judgments walk for evermore.

A Hymn to Christ . . .

JOHN DONNE (English, 1572–1631)

In what torn ship soever I embark,
That ship shall be my emblem of thy ark;
What sea soever swallow me, that flood
Shall be to me an emblem of thy blood;
Though thou with clouds of anger do disguise
Thy face, yet through that mask I know those eyes,
  Which, though they turn away sometimes,
    They never will despise.

I sacrifice this Island unto thee,
And all whom I love there, and who loved me;
When I have put our seas 'twixt them and me,
Put thou thy seas betwixt my sins and thee.
As the tree's sap doth seek the root below
In winter, in my winter now I go,
  Where none but thee, the eternal root
    Of true love, I may know.

Nor thou nor thy religion dost control
The amorousness of an harmonious soul;
But thou wouldst have that love thyself: as thou
Art jealous, Lord, so I am jealous now;
Thou lov'st not, till from loving more, thou free
My soul; who ever gives, takes liberty:
  O, if thou car'st not whom I love,
    Alas, thou lov'st not me.

Seal then this bill of my divorce to all,
On whom those fainter beams of love did fall;
Marry those loves, which in youth scattered be
On fame, wit, hopes (false mistresses) to thee.
Churches are best for prayer, that have least light;
To see God only, I go out of sight:
  And to escape stormy days, I choose
    An everlasting night.

FROM *Moby Dick*

HERMAN MELVILLE (American, 1819–1891)

[Editor's note: *Moby Dick* is called the great American novel, though many of us have read only the abridged version—which often doesn't include this blustery, eloquent sermon on Jonah by the priest of the Whaleman's Chapel in New Bedford. Here the priest speaks not only prophetically, but out of the depths of his own unnamed suffering.]

Father Mapple rose, and in a mild voice of unassuming authority ordered the scattered people to condense. "Starboard gangway, there! side way to larboard—larboard gangway, to starboard! Midships! midships!"

There was a low rumbling of heavy sea-boots among the benches, and a still slighter shuffling of women's shoes, and all was quiet again, and every eye on the preacher.

He paused a little; then kneeling in the pulpit's bows, folded his large brown hands across his chest, uplifted his closed eyes, and offered a prayer so deeply devout that he seemed kneeling and praying at the bottom of the sea. . . .

. . . A brief pause ensued; the preacher slowly turned over the leaves of the Bible, and at last, folding his hand down upon the proper page, said: "Beloved shipmates, clinch the last verse of the first chapter of Jonah—'And God had prepared a great fish to swallow up Jonah.'"

"Shipmates, this book, containing only four chapters—four yarns—is one of the smallest strands in the mighty cable of the Scriptures. Yet what depths of the soul does Jonah's deep sea-line sound! what a pregnant lesson to us is this prophet! What a noble thing is that canticle in the fish's belly! How billow-like and boisterously grand! We feel the floods surging over us; we sound with him to the kelpy bottom of the waters; sea-weed and all the slime of the sea is about us! But *what* is this lesson that the book of Jonah teaches? Shipmates, it is a two-stranded lesson; a lesson to us all as sinful men, and a lesson to me as a pilot of the living God. As sinful men, it is a lesson to us all, because it is a story of the sin, hard-heartedness, suddenly awakened fears, the swift punishment, repentance, prayers and finally the deliverance and joy of Jonah. As with all sinners among men, the sin of this son of Amittai was in his willful disobedience to the command of God—never mind now what that command was, or how conveyed—which he found a hard command. But all the things that God would have us do are hard for us to do—remember that—and hence, He oftener commands us than endeavors to persuade. And if we obey God, we must disobey ourselves; and it is in this disobeying ourselves, wherein the hardness of obeying God consists."

[continued below]

FROM *Moby Dick*

"And now behold Jonah taken up as an anchor and dropped into the sea; when instantly an oily calmness floats out from the east, and the sea is still, as Jonah carries down the gale with him, leaving smooth water behind. He goes down in the whirling heart of such a masterless commotion that he scarce heeds the moment when he drops seething into the yawning jaws awaiting him; and the whale shoots-to all his ivory teeth, like so many white bolts, upon his prison. Then Jonah prayed unto the Lord out of the fish's belly. But observe his prayer, and learn a weighty lesson. For sinful as he is, Jonah does not weep and wail for direct deliverance. He feels that his dreadful punishment is just. He leaves all his deliverance to God, contenting himself with this, that spite of all his pains and pangs, he will still look towards His holy temple. And here shipmates, is true and faithful repentance; not clamorous for pardon, but grateful for punishment. And how pleasing to God was this conduct in Jonah, is shown in the eventual deliverance of him from the sea and the whale. Shipmates, I do not place Jonah before you to be copied for his sin but I do place him before you as a model for repentance. Sin not; but if you do, take heed to repent of it like Jonah."

While he was speaking these words, the howling of the shrieking, slanting storm without seemed to add new power to the preacher, who, when describing Jonah's sea-storm, seemed tossed by a storm himself. His deep chest heaved as with a ground-swell; his tossed arms seemed the warring elements at work; and the thunders that rolled away from off his swarthy brow, and the light leaping from his eye, made all his simple hearers look on him with a quick fear that was strange to them.

WEEK 13

Compelled by Mercy

OPENING PRAYER

As froth on the face of the deep,
As foam on the crest of the sea,
As dreams at the waking of sleep,
As gourd of a day and a night,
As harvest that no man shall reap
As vintage that never shall be,
Is hope if it cling not aright
O my God, unto Thee.
—CHRISTINA ROSSETTI (English, 1830–1894)

SCRIPTURES

PSALM 51 | JONAH 3:1–10 | ACTS 2:37–42 | LUKE 7:36–50

READINGS

"A Hymn to God the Father" by JOHN DONNE
"The Hazelnut" by JULIAN OF NORWICH
From "The Weeper" by RICHARD CRASHAW
"Church-Lock and Key" by GEORGE HERBERT
From *Moby Dick* by HERMAN MELVILLE

PERSONAL PRAYER AND REFLECTION

CLOSING PRAYER

Enough, enough we mourn!
Let us no more return
Repulsed with blame and shame from thee;

But succor us oppressed
And give the troubled rest
That of thy praise their songs may be.
—MARY HERBERT (English, 1561–1621)

READINGS FOR WEEK 13

A Hymn to God the Father

JOHN DONNE (English, 1571–1631)

I.
Wilt thou forgive that sin where I begun,
Which was my sin, though it were done before?
Wilt thou forgive that sin, through which I run,
And do run still: though still I do deplore?
When thou hast done, thou hast not done,
For, I have more.

II.
Wilt thou forgive that sin which I have won
Others to sin? and, made my sin their door?
Wilt thou forgive that sin which I did shun
A year, or two: but wallowed in, a score?
When thou hast done, thou hast not done,
For I have more.

III.
I have a sin of fear, that when I have spun
My last thread, I shall perish on the shore;
But swear by thy self, that at my death thy son
Shall shine as it shines now, and heretofore;
And, having done that, thou hast done,
I fear no more.

The Hazelnut

(ADAPTED FROM *Revelations of Divine Love*)

JULIAN OF NORWICH (English, ca. 1342–ca. 1416)

He showed me
a little thing,
the quantity of a hazelnut,
in the palm of my hand;
and it was as round as a ball.
I looked upon it
with my inner eye of understanding,
and thought: What may this be?
And it was answered:
  It is all that is made.
I marveled how it could last,
for I thought it might suddenly
fall to nothing for littleness.
And I was answered in my understanding:
  It lasts,
  and ever shall last
  because God loves it.
And so All-thing has Being
by the love of God.

In this Little Thing
I saw three properties.
The first is that God made it,
the second is that God loves it,
the third, that God keeps it.
But what is to me
indeed, the Maker, the Keeper, and the Lover—
I cannot tell; for till I am
substantially oned to Him,

I may never have full rest
nor bliss: that is to say,
till I be so fastened to Him,
there is nothing that is made
between my God and me.

FROM *"The Weeper"*

RICHARD CRASHAW (English, 1613–1649)

O precious Prodigal!
Fair spend-thrift of thy self! thy measure
(merciless love) is all
Even to the last pearl in thy treasure.
All places, times, and objects be
Thy tear's sweet opportunity.

Does the daystar rise?
Still thy stars do fall and fall.
Does day close his eyes?
Still the fountain weeps for all.
Let night or day do what they will,
Thou hast thy task; thou weepest still.

Does thy song lull the air?
Thy falling tears keep faith full time.
Does thy sweet-breath'd prayer
Up in clouds of incense climb?
Still at each sigh, that is, each stop,
A bead, that is, a tear, does drop.

At these thy weeping gates,
(watching their watry motion)

Each winged moment waits,
Takes his tear, and gets him gone.
By thine eye's tinct enobled thus
Time lays him up; he's precious.

Not, so long she lived,
Shall thy tomb report of thee;
But, so long she grieved,
Thus must we date thy memory.
Others by moments, months, and years,
Measure their ages; thou, by tears.

Church-Lock and Key

GEORGE HERBERT (English, 1593–1633)

I know it is my sin, which locks thine ears,
And binds thy hands,
Out-crying my requests, drowning my tears;
Or else the chillness of my faint demands.

But as cold hands are angry with the fire,
And mend it still;
So I do lay the want of my desire,
Not on my sins, or coldness, but thy will.

Yet hear, O God, only for his blood's sake
Which pleads for me:
For though sins plead too, yet like stones they make
His blood's sweat current much more loud to be.

From *Moby Dick*

Herman Melville (American, 1819–1891)

[Editor's note: Here we pick up where last week's reading left off, continuing the sermon on Jonah by Father Mapple, priest of the Whaleman's Chapel in New Bedford. His sermon concludes with a powerful appeal to God's mercy for the repentant sinner.]

There now came a lull in [Father Mapple's] look, as he silently turned over the leaves of the Book once more; and, at last, standing motionless, with closed eyes, for the moment, seemed communing with God and himself.

But again he leaned over towards the people, and bowing his head lowly, with an aspect of the deepest yet manliest humility, he spake these words:

"Shipmates, God has laid but one hand upon you; both his hands press upon me. I have read ye by what murky light may be mine the lesson that Jonah teaches to all sinners; and therefore to ye, and still more to me, for I am a greater sinner than ye. And now how gladly would I come down from this mast-head and sit on the hatches there where you sit, and listen as you listen, while some one of you reads *me* that other and more awful lesson which Jonah teaches to *me*, as a pilot of the living God. How being an anointed pilot-prophet, or speaker of true things, and bidden by the Lord to sound those unwelcome truths in the ears of a wicked Nineveh, Jonah, appalled at the hostility he should raise, fled from his mission, and sought to escape his duty and his God by taking ship at Joppa. But God is everywhere; Tarshish he never reached. As we have seen, God came upon him in the whale, and swallowed him down to living gulfs of doom, and with swift slantings tore him along 'into the midst of the seas,' where the eddying depths sucked him ten thousand fathoms down, and 'the weeds were wrapped about his head,' and all the watery world of woe bowled over him. Yet even then beyond the reach of any plummet—'out of the belly of hell'—when the whale grounded upon the ocean's utmost bones, even then, God heard the engulfed, repenting prophet when he cried. Then God spake unto the fish; and from the shuddering cold and blackness of the sea, the whale came breeching up towards the warm and pleasant sun, and all the delights of air and earth; and 'vomited out Jonah upon the dry land;' when the word of the Lord came a second time; and Jonah, bruised and beaten—his ears, like two sea-shells, still multitudinously murmuring of the ocean—Jonah did the Almighty's bidding. And what was that, shipmates? To preach the Truth to the face of Falsehood! That was it!"

[continued below]

FROM *Moby Dick*

"This, shipmates, this is that other lesson; and woe to the pilot of the living God who slights it. Woe to him whom this world charms from Gospel Duty! Woe to him who seeks to pour oil upon the waters when God has brewed them into a gale! Woe to him who seeks to please rather than to appall! Woe to him whose good name is more to him than goodness! Woe to him who, in this world, courts not dishonor! Woe to him who would not be true, even though to be false were salvation! Yea, woe to him who, as the great Pilot Paul has it, while preaching to others is himself a castaway!"

He drooped and fell away from himself for a moment; then lifting his face to them again, showed a deep joy in his eyes, as he cried out with a heavenly enthusiasm,—"But oh! shipmates! on the starboard hand of every woe, there is a sure delight; and higher the top of that delight, than the bottom of the woe is deep.

Is not the main-truck higher than the keelson is low? Delight is to him—a far, far upward, and inward delight—who against the proud gods and commodores of this earth, ever stands forth his own inexorable self. Delight is to him whose strong arms yet support him, when the ship of this base treacherous world has gone down beneath him. Delight is to him, who gives no quarter in the truth, and kills, burns, and destroys all sin though he pluck it out from under the robes of Senators and Judges. Delight—top-gallant delight is to him, who acknowledges no law or lord, but the Lord his God, and is only a patriot to heaven. Delight is to him, whom all the waves of the billows of the seas of the boisterous mob can never shake from this sure Keel of the Ages. And eternal delight and deliciousness will be his, who coming to lay him down, can say with his final breath—O Father!—chiefly known to me by Thy rod—mortal or immortal, here I die. I have striven to be Thine, more than to be this world's, or mine own. Yet this is nothing; I leave eternity to Thee; for what is man that he should live out the lifetime of his God?"

He said no more, but slowly waving a benediction, covered his face with his hands, and so remained kneeling, till all the people had departed, and he was left alone in the place.

WEEK 14

Ransomed for Good

OPENING PRAYER

Thou art my God, I know,
My King, who long ago
Didst undertake the charge of me;
And in my hard distress
Didst work me such release
That all the earth did wondering see.
—MARY HERBERT (English, 1561–1621)

SCRIPTURES

PSALM 32 | ISAIAH 44:21–28 | 1 PETER 1:17–25 | LUKE 15:11–32

READINGS

"Love (III)" by GEORGE HERBERT
"Transformation" by ANNA KAMIEŃSKA
From *Les Misérables* by VICTOR HUGO

PERSONAL PRAYER AND REFLECTION

CLOSING PRAYER

O my Savior, make me see
How dearly thou hast paid for me

That lost again my life may prove
As then in death, so now in love.
—RICHARD CRASHAW (English, 1613–1649)

READINGS FOR WEEK 14

Love (III)

George Herbert (English, 1593–1633)

Love bade me welcome: yet my soul drew back,
Guilty of dust and sin.
But quick-eyed Love, observing me grow slack
From my first entrance in,
Drew nearer to me, sweetly questioning
If I lacked any thing.

A guest, I answered, worthy to be here:
Love said, You shall be he.
I the unkind, ungrateful? Ah my dear,
I cannot look on thee.
Love took my hand and smiling did reply,
Who made the eyes but I?

Truth, Lord, but I have marred them; let my shame
Go where it doth deserve.
And know you not, says Love, who bore the blame?
My dear, then I will serve.
You must sit down, says Love, and taste my meat:
So I did sit and eat.

Transformation

Anna Kamieńska (Polish, 1920–1986)

To be transformed
to turn yourself inside out like a glove
to spin like a planet
to thread yourself through yourself
so that each day penetrates each night
so that each word runs to the other side of truth
so that each verse comes out of itself
and gives off its own light
so that each face leaning on a hand
sweats into the skin of the palm

So that this pen
changes into pure silence
I wanted to say into love

To fall off a horse
to smear your face with dust
to be blinded
to lift yourself
and allow yourself to be led
like blind Saul
to Damascus

From *Les Misérables*

Victor Hugo (French, 1802–1885)

[Editor's note: In Hugo's masterpiece, the convict Jean Valjean, after having been sentenced to hard labor for stealing bread, is finally released, only to nearly starve on the streets. He is given food and shelter by the local Bishop Bienvenu (a name meaning "welcome"), the bishop's sister, and his housekeeper, Madame Magloire—hospitality Jean repays by stealing the bishop's silver and running away. The bishop's response is perhaps one of the most poignant moments of redemption in all literature.]

The next morning at sunrise Monsignor Bienvenu was strolling in his garden. Madame Magloire ran up to him in utter consternation.

"Monsignor, Monsignor!" she exclaimed, "does your Grace know where the basket of silver is?"

"Yes," replied the Bishop.

"Jesus the Lord be blessed!" she resumed; "I did not know what had become of it."

The Bishop had just picked up the basket in a flower-bed. He presented it to Madame Magloire.

"Here it is."

"Well!" said she. "Nothing in it! And the silver?"

"Ah," returned the Bishop, "so it is the silver which troubles you? I don't know where it is."

"Great, good God! It is stolen! That man who was here last night has stolen it."

In a twinkling, with all the vivacity of an alert old woman, Madame Magloire had rushed to the oratory, entered the alcove, and returned to the Bishop. The Bishop had just bent down, and was sighing as he examined a plant of *cochlearia des Guillons*, which the basket had broken as it fell across the bed. He rose up at Madame Magloire's cry.

"Monsignor, the man is gone! The silver has been stolen!"

As she uttered this exclamation, her eyes fell upon a corner of the garden, where traces of the wall having been scaled were visible. The coping of the wall had been torn away.

"Stay! yonder is the way he went. He jumped over into Cochefilet Lane. Ah, the abomination! He has stolen our silver!"

The Bishop remained silent for a moment; then he raised his grave eyes, and said gently to Madame Magloire:—

"And, in the first place, was that silver ours?"

[continued below]

FROM *Les Misérables*

. . . Madame Magloire was speechless. Another silence ensued; then the Bishop went on:—

"Madame Magloire, I have for a long time detained that silver wrongfully. It belonged to the poor. Who was that man? A poor man, evidently."

"Alas! Jesus!" returned Madame Magloire. "It is not for my sake, nor for Mademoiselle's. It makes no difference to us. But it is for the sake of Monsignor. What is Monsignor to eat with now?"

The Bishop gazed at her with an air of amazement.

"Ah, come! Are there no such things as pewter forks and spoons?"

Madame Magloire shrugged her shoulders.

"Pewter has an odor."

"Iron forks and spoons, then."

Madame Magloire made an expressive grimace.

"Iron has a taste."

"Very well," said the Bishop; "wooden ones then."

A few moments later he was breakfasting at the very table at which Jean Valjean had sat on the previous evening. As he ate his breakfast, Monsignor Bienvenu remarked gayly to his sister, who said nothing, and to Madame Magloire, who was grumbling under her breath, that one really does not need either fork or spoon, even of wood, in order to dip a bit of bread in a cup of milk.

"A pretty idea, truly," said Madame Magloire to herself, as she went and came, "to take in a man like that! and to lodge him close to one's self! And how fortunate that he did nothing but steal! Ah, *mon Dieu*! it makes one shudder to think of it!"

As the brother and sister were about to rise from the table, there came a knock at the door.

"Come in," said the Bishop.

The door opened. A singular and violent group made its appearance on the threshold. Three men were holding a fourth man by the collar. The three men were gendarmes; the other was Jean Valjean.

A brigadier of gendarmes, who seemed to be in command of the group, was standing near the door. He entered and advanced to the Bishop, making a military salute.

"Monsignor—" said he.

At this word, Jean Valjean, who was dejected and seemed overwhelmed, raised his head with an air of stupefaction.

"Monsignor!" he murmured. "So he is not the cure?"

"Silence!" said the gendarme. "He is Monsignor the Bishop."

In the meantime, Monsignor Bienvenu had advanced as quickly as his great age permitted.

"Ah! here you are!" he exclaimed, looking at Jean Valjean. "I am glad to see you. Well, but how is this? I gave you the candlesticks too, which are of silver like the rest, and for which you can certainly get two hundred francs. Why did you not carry them away with your forks and spoons?"

[continued below]

———

From *Les Misérables*

Jean Valjean opened his eyes wide, and stared at the venerable Bishop with an expression which no human tongue can render any account of.

"Monsignor," said the brigadier of gendarmes, "so what this man said is true, then? We came across him. He was walking like a man who is running away. We stopped him to look into the matter. He had this silver—"

"And he told you," interposed the Bishop with a smile, "that it had been given to him by a kind old fellow of a priest with whom he had passed the night? I see how the matter stands. And you have brought him back here? It is a mistake."

"In that case," replied the brigadier, "we can let him go?"

"Certainly," replied the Bishop.

The gendarmes released Jean Valjean, who recoiled.

"Is it true that I am to be released?" he said, in an almost inarticulate voice, and as though he were talking in his sleep.

"Yes, thou art released; dost thou not understand?" said one of the gendarmes.

"My friend," resumed the Bishop, "before you go, here are your candlesticks. Take them."

He stepped to the chimney-piece, took the two silver candlesticks, and brought them to Jean Valjean. The two women looked on without uttering a word, without a gesture, without a look which could disconcert the Bishop.

Jean Valjean was trembling in every limb. He took the two candlesticks mechanically, and with a bewildered air.

"Now," said the Bishop, "go in peace. By the way, when you return, my friend, it is not necessary to pass through the garden. You can always enter and depart through the street door. It is never fastened with anything but a latch, either by day or by night."

Then, turning to the gendarmes:—

"You may retire, gentlemen."

The gendarmes retired.

Jean Valjean was like a man on the point of fainting.

The Bishop drew near to him, and said in a low voice:—

"Do not forget, never forget, that you have promised to use this money in becoming an honest man."

Jean Valjean, who had no recollection of ever having promised anything, remained speechless. The Bishop had emphasized the words when he uttered them. He resumed with solemnity:—

"Jean Valjean, my brother, you no longer belong to evil, but to good. It is your soul that I buy from you; I withdraw it from black thoughts and the spirit of perdition, and I give it to God."

WEEK 15

Bending the Knee

OPENING PRAYER

Half-starved of soul and heartsick utterly,
  Yet lift I up my heart and soul and eyes
  (Which fail in looking upward) toward the prize:
Me, Lord, Thou seest though I see not Thee;
  Me now, as once the Thief in Paradise,
Even me, O Lord my Lord, remember me.
—CHRISTINA ROSSETTI (English, 1830–1894)

SCRIPTURES

PSALM 107 | ISAIAH 30:15–26 | 2 CORINTHIANS 7:8–12 |
LUKE 23:32–43

READINGS

"Adventures in New Testament Greek: *Metanoia*" by SCOTT CAIRNS
From "The Ballad of Reading Gaol"[10] by OSCAR WILDE
From *Crime and Punishment* by FYODOR DOSTOEVSKY

PERSONAL PRAYER AND REFLECTION

CLOSING PRAYER

Search me, my God, and prove my heart,
  Examine me, and try my thought;
    And mark in me
    If aught there be
  That hath with cause their anger wrought.

10 *gaol*—an alternate spelling of "jail."

If not (as not) my life's each part,
Lord, safely guide from danger brought.
—Mary Herbert (English, 1561–1621)

READINGS FOR WEEK 15

Adventures in New Testament Greek: Metanoia

Scott Cairns (American, contemporary)

Repentance, to be sure,
but of a species far
less likely to oblige
sheepish repetition.

Repentance, you'll observe,
glibly bears the bent
of thought revisited,
and mind's familiar stamp

—a quaint, half-hearted
doubleness that couples
all compunction with a pledge
of recurrent screw-up.

The heart's *metanoia*,
on the other hand, turns
without regret, turns not
so much *away*, as *toward*,

as if the slow pilgrim
has been surprised to find
that sin is not so bad
as it is a waste of time.

———

FROM *"The Ballad of Reading Gaol"*
OSCAR WILDE (Irish, 1854–1900)

. . . And thus we rust Life's iron chain
  Degraded and alone:
And some men curse, and some men weep,
  And some men make no moan:
But God's eternal Laws are kind
  And break the heart of stone.

And every human heart that breaks,
  In prison-cell or yard,
Is as that broken box that gave
  Its treasure to the Lord,
And filled the unclean leper's house
  With the scent of costliest nard.

Ah! happy they whose hearts can break
  And peace of pardon win!
How else may man make straight his plan
  And cleanse his soul from Sin?
How else but through a broken heart
  May Lord Christ enter in?

FROM the Epilogue of *Crime and Punishment*
FYODOR DOSTOEVSKY (Russian, 1821–1881)

[Editor's note: In the epilogue of Dostoevsky's *Crime and Punishment*, the murderer Raskolnikov is serving a prison sentence in Siberia, still unrepentant but resigned. Meanwhile the former prostitute Sofya Semyonovna (Sonia)—a broken woman of great faith—has followed him and awaits both his release from prison and his genuine repentance.]

One evening, when he was almost well again, Raskolnikov fell asleep. On waking up he chanced to go to the window, and at once saw Sonia in the distance at the hospital gate. She seemed to be waiting for someone. Something stabbed him to the heart at that minute. He shuddered and moved away from the window. Next day Sonia did not come, nor the day after; he noticed that he was expecting her uneasily. At last he was discharged. On reaching the prison he learnt from the convicts that Sofya Semyonovna was lying ill at home and was unable to go out.

He was very uneasy and sent to inquire after her; he soon learnt that her illness was not dangerous. Hearing that he was anxious about her, Sonia sent him a penciled note, telling him that she was much better, that she had a slight cold and that she would soon, very soon come and see him at his work. His heart throbbed painfully as he read it.

Again it was a warm bright day. Early in the morning, at six o'clock, he went off to work on the river bank, where they used to pound alabaster and where there was a kiln for baking it in a shed. There were only three of them sent. One of the convicts went with the guard to the fortress to fetch a tool; the other began getting the wood ready and laying it in the kiln. Raskolnikov came out of the shed on to the river bank, sat down on a heap of logs by the shed and began gazing at the wide deserted river. From the high bank a broad landscape opened before him, the sound of singing floated faintly audible from the other bank. In the vast steppe, bathed in sunshine, he could just see, like black specks, the nomads' tents. There there was freedom, there other men were living, utterly unlike those here; there time itself seemed to stand still, as though the age of Abraham and his flocks had not passed. Raskolnikov sat gazing, his thoughts passed into day-dreams, into contemplation; he thought of nothing, but a vague restlessness excited and troubled him. Suddenly he found Sonia beside him; she had come up noiselessly and sat down at his side. It was still quite early; the morning chill was still keen. She wore her poor old burnous and the green shawl; her face still showed signs of illness, it was thinner and paler. She gave him a joyful smile of welcome, but held out her hand with her usual timidity. She was always timid of holding out her hand to him and sometimes did not offer it at all, as though afraid he would repel it. He always took her hand as though with repugnance, always seemed vexed to meet her and was sometimes obstinately silent throughout her visit. Sometimes she trembled before him and went away deeply grieved. But now their hands did not part. He stole a rapid glance at her and dropped his eyes on the ground without speaking. They were alone, no one had seen them. The guard had turned away for the time.

How it happened he did not know. But all at once something seemed to seize him and fling him at her feet. He wept and threw his arms round her knees. For the first instant she was terribly frightened and she turned pale. She jumped up and looked at him trembling. But at the same moment she understood, and a light of infinite happiness came into her eyes. She knew and had no doubt that he loved her beyond everything and that at last the moment had come.

[continued below]

FROM the Epilogue of *Crime and Punishment*

They wanted to speak, but could not; tears stood in their eyes. They were both pale and thin; but those sick pale faces were bright with the dawn of a new future, of a full resurrection into a new life. They were renewed by love; the heart of each held infinite sources of life for the heart of the other.

They resolved to wait and be patient. They had another seven years to wait, and what terrible suffering and what infinite happiness before them! But he had risen again and he knew it and felt it in all his being, while she—she only lived in his life.

On the evening of the same day, when the barracks were locked, Raskolnikov lay on his plank bed and thought of her. He had even fancied that day that all the convicts who had been his enemies looked at him differently; he had even entered into talk with them and they answered him in a friendly way. He remembered that now, and thought it was bound to be so. Wasn't everything now bound to be changed?

He thought of her. He remembered how continually he had tormented her and wounded her heart. He remembered her pale and thin little face. But these recollections scarcely troubled him now; he knew with what infinite love he would now repay all her sufferings. And what were all, *all* the agonies of the past! Everything, even his crime, his sentence and imprisonment, seemed to him now in the first rush of feeling an external, strange fact with which he had no concern. But he could not think for long together of anything that evening, and he could not have analyzed anything consciously; he was simply feeling. Life had stepped into the place of theory and something quite different would work itself out in his mind.

Under his pillow lay the New Testament. He took it up mechanically. The book belonged to Sonia; it was the one from which she had read the raising of Lazarus to him. At first he was afraid that she would worry him about religion, would talk about the gospel and pester him with books. But to his great surprise she had not once approached the subject and had not even offered him the Testament. He had asked her for it himself not long before his illness and she brought him the book without a word. Till now he had not opened it.

He did not open it now, but one thought passed through his mind: "Can her convictions not be mine now? Her feelings, her aspirations at least. . . ."

She too had been greatly agitated that day, and at night she was taken ill again. But she was so happy—and so unexpectedly happy—that she was almost frightened of her happiness. Seven years, *only* seven years! At the beginning of their happiness at some moments they were both ready to look on those seven years as though they were seven days. He did not know that the new life would not be given him for nothing, that he would have to pay dearly for it, that it would cost him great striving, great suffering.

But that is the beginning of a new story—the story of the gradual renewal of a man, the story of his gradual regeneration, of his passing from one world into another, of his initiation into a new unknown life. That might be the subject of a new story, but our present story is ended.

WEEK 16

Fresh Vision

OPENING PRAYER

Lord, purge our eyes to see
Within the seed a tree
  Within the glowing egg a bird,
    Within the shroud a butterfly:

Till taught by such, we see
Beyond all creatures Thee;
  And hearken for Thy tender word,
    And hear it, "Fear not: it is I."
—CHRISTINA ROSSETTI (English, 1830–1894)

SCRIPTURES

PSALM 95 | 1 SAMUEL 2:1–10 | ROMANS 8:31–39 | JOHN 2:1–11

READINGS

"Morning Reflections" by ENUMA OKORO
"Contemplations (I and II)" by ANNE BRADSTREET
"Pied Beauty" by GERARD MANLEY HOPKINS
"Gratitude" by ANNA KAMIEŃSKA
From *The Brothers Karamazov* by FYODOR DOSTOEVSKY

PERSONAL PRAYER AND REFLECTION

CLOSING PRAYER

Thy word and wisdom Thou
To lighten man hast given,
That he the splendor might reflect

That shines superb in heaven;
And having light within,
Might see Thine image bright,
And daily rise, till he himself
Is altogether light.
—adapted from the poetry of GREGORY OF NAZIANZUS (Cappadocia/modern-day Turkey, AD 325–390)

READINGS FOR WEEK 16

Morning Reflections

ENUMA OKORO (Nigerian-American, contemporary)

What is this unfolding, this slow-
going unraveling of gift held
in hands open
to the wonder and enchantment of it all?

What is this growing, this rare
showing, like blossoming
of purple spotted forests
by roadsides grown weary with winter months?

Seasons affected, routinely disordered
by playful disturbance of divine glee
weaving through limbs with
sharpened shards of mirrored light,
cutting dark spaces, interlacing creation,
commanding life with whimsical delight.

What is this breaking, this hopeful
re-making, shifting stones, addressing dry bones,

dizzying me with blessings,
intercepting my grieving
and raising the dead all around me?

Contemplations (I and II)

ANNE BRADSTREET (English-American, 1612–1672)

I.
Some time now past in the autumnal tide,
When Phoebus[11] wanted but one hour to bed,
The trees all richly clad, yet void of pride,
Were gilded o'er by his rich golden head;
Their leaves and fruits seemed painted, but was true,
Of green, of red, of yellow, mixèd hue;
Rapt were my senses at this delectable view.

II.
I wist not what to wish. Yet sure, thought I,
If so much excellence abide below,
How excellent is He that dwells on high?
Whose power and beauty by His works we know!
Sure He is goodness, wisdom, glory, light,
That hath this under-world so richly dight.[12]
More heaven than earth was here, no winter and no night.

---

11 *Phoebus*—another name for the Greek god Helios, or the sun.

12 *dight*—adorned or dressed.

Pied Beauty

GERARD MANLEY HOPKINS (English, 1844–1889)

Glory be to God for dappled things—
    For skies of couple-color as a brindled cow;
        For rose-moles all in stipple upon trout that swim;
Fresh-firecoal chestnut-falls; finches' wings;
    Landscapes plotted and pieced—fold, fallow, and plough;
        And all trades, their gear and tackle and trim.

All things counter, original, spare, strange;
    Whatever is fickle, freckled (who knows how?)
        With swift, slow; sweet, sour; adazzle, dim;
He fathers-forth whose beauty is past change:
                                        Praise him.

Gratitude

ANNA KAMIEŃSKA (Polish, 1920–1986)

A tempest threw a rainbow in my face
so that I wanted to fall under the rain
to kiss the hands of an old woman to whom I gave my seat
to thank everyone for the fact that they exist
and at times even feel like smiling
I was grateful to young leaves that they were willing
to open up to the sun
to babies that they still
felt like coming into this world
to the old that they heroically
endure until the end
I was full of thanks

like a Sunday alms-box
I would have embraced death
if she'd stopped nearby

Gratitude is a scattered
homeless love

From *The Brothers Karamazov*

Fyodor Dostoevsky (Russian, 1821–1881)

[Editor's note: Alyosha, the youngest son of the scoundrel Fyodor Karamazov, rejects his father's wicked ways by becoming a monk and finding a new father figure in Zossima, elder of the local monastery. But Father Zossima dies, leaving Alyosha bereft. Here, during the elder's funeral wake, the young monk falls into a trance, dreaming that he and the elder are at the wedding banquet in John 2. The vision stirs Alyosha to greater hope and love for the world.]

It was his voice, the voice of Father Zossima. And it must be he, since he called him!

The elder raised Alyosha by the hand and he rose from his knees.

"We are rejoicing," the little, thin old man went on. "We are drinking the new wine, the wine of new, great gladness; do you see how many guests? Here are the bride and bridegroom, here is the wise governor of the feast, he is tasting the new wine. Why do you wonder at me? I gave an onion to a beggar, so I, too, am here. And many here have given only an onion each—only one little onion. . . . What are all our deeds? And you, my gentle one, you, my kind boy, you too have known how to give a famished woman an onion today. Begin your work, dear one, begin it, gentle one! Do you see our Sun, do you see Him?"

"I am afraid . . . I dare not look," whispered Alyosha.

"Do not fear Him. He is terrible in His greatness, awful in His sublimity, but infinitely merciful. He has made Himself like unto us from love and rejoices with us. He is changing the water into wine that the gladness of the guests may not be cut short. He is expecting new guests, He is calling new ones unceasingly for ever and ever. . . . There they are bringing new wine. Do you see they are bringing the vessels . . ."

Something glowed in Alyosha's heart, something filled it till it ached, tears of rapture rose from his soul. . . . He stretched out his hands, uttered a cry and waked up.

Again the coffin, the open window, and the soft, solemn, distinct reading of the Gospel. But Alyosha did not listen to the reading. It was strange, he had fallen asleep on his knees, but now he was on his feet, and suddenly, as though thrown forward, with three firm rapid steps he went right up to the coffin. His shoulder brushed against Father Paissy without his noticing it. Father Paissy raised his eyes for an instant from his book, but looked away again at once, seeing that something strange was happening to the boy. Alyosha gazed for half a minute at the coffin, at the covered, motionless dead man that lay in the coffin, with the icon on his breast and the peaked cap with the octangular cross on his head. He had only just been hearing his voice, and that voice was still ringing in his ears. He was listening, still expecting other words, but suddenly he turned sharply and went out of the cell.

[continued below]

FROM *The Brothers Karamazov*

He did not stop on the steps either, but went quickly down; his soul, overflowing with rapture, yearned for freedom, space, openness. The vault of heaven, full of soft, shining stars, stretched vast and fathomless above him. The Milky Way ran in two pale streams from the zenith to the horizon. The fresh, motionless, still night enfolded the earth. The white towers and golden domes of the cathedral gleamed out against the sapphire sky. The gorgeous autumn flowers, in the beds round the house, were slumbering till morning. The silence of earth seemed to melt into the silence of the heavens. The mystery of earth was one with the mystery of the stars. . . .

Alyosha stood, gazed, and suddenly threw himself down on the earth. He did not know why he embraced it. He could not have told why he longed so irresistibly to kiss it, to kiss it all. But he kissed it weeping, sobbing, and watering it with his tears, and vowed passionately to love it, to love it for ever and ever. "Water the earth with the tears of your joy and love those tears," echoed in his soul.

What was he weeping over?

Oh! in his rapture he was weeping even over those stars, which were shining to him from the abyss of space, and "he was not ashamed of that ecstasy." There seemed to be threads from all those innumerable worlds of God, linking his soul to them, and it was trembling all over "in contact with other worlds." He longed to forgive everyone and for everything, and to beg forgiveness. Oh, not for himself, but for all men, for all and for everything. "And others are praying for me too," echoed again in his soul. But with every instant he felt clearly and, as it were, tangibly, that something firm and unshakable as that vault of heaven had entered into his soul. It was as though some idea had seized the sovereignty of his mind—and it was for all his life and for ever and ever. He had fallen on the earth a weak boy, but he rose up a resolute champion, and he knew and felt it suddenly at the very moment of his ecstasy. And never, never, his life long, could Alyosha forget that minute.

"Someone visited my soul in that hour," he used to say afterwards, with implicit faith in his words.

Within three days he left the monastery in accordance with the words of his elder, who had bidden him "sojourn in the world."

WEEK 17

Called by God

OPENING PRAYER

Almighty God, who presses Your divine summons upon frail and flawed human beings; grant that we, though small of heart and hard of hearing, may seek Your face and obey Your voice; through the obedience of Jesus Christ our Lord, *Amen.*

SCRIPTURES

Psalm 33 | Exodus 3:1–12 | Acts 12:1–17 | Luke 1:26–38

READINGS

From "St. Peter's Day" by John Keble
"Upon the Annunciation and Passion falling upon one day. 1608" by John Donne
From "The Call of the Christian" by John Greenleaf Whittier
From *The Man Who Was Thursday* by G. K. Chesterton

PERSONAL PRAYER AND REFLECTION

CLOSING PRAYER

The smiles of earth that turn to tears,
Its empty joys and foolish fears
I leave, for Thou dost call—
Thou art my Life, my All.
—adapted from the poetry of Methodius
(Mediterranean, third century AD)

READINGS FOR WEEK 17

FROM *"St. Peter's Day"* in *The Christian Year*
JOHN KEBLE (English, 1792–1866)

He dreams he sees a lamp flash bright,
  Glancing around his prison room—
But 'tis a gleam of heavenly light
  That fills up all the ample gloom.

The flame, that in a few short years
  Deep through the chambers of the dead
Shall pierce, and dry the fount of tears,
  Is waving o'er his dungeon-bed.

Touched he upstarts—his chains unbind—
  Through darksome vault, up massy stair,
His dizzy, doubting footsteps wind
  To freedom and cool moonlight air.

Then all himself, all joy and calm,
  Though for a while his hand forego,
Just as it touched, the martyr's palm,
  He turns him to his task below;

The pastoral staff, the keys of Heaven,
  To wield a while in grey-haired might,
Then from his cross to spring forgiven,
  And follow JESUS out of sight.

FROM *"Upon the Annunciation and Passion falling upon one day. 1608"*
JOHN DONNE (English, 1572–1631)

Tamely, frail body, abstain today; today
My soul eats twice, Christ hither and away.
She sees him man, so like God made in this,
That of them both a circle emblem is,
Whose first and last concur; this doubtful day
Of feast or fast, Christ came, and went away;
She sees him nothing twice at once, who is all;
She sees a cedar plant itself, and fall;
Her maker put to making, and the head
Of life, at once, not yet alive, and dead;
She sees at once the virgin mother stay
Reclused at home, public at Golgotha;
Sad and rejoiced she's seen at once, and seen
At almost fifty, and at scarce fifteen;
At once a son is promised her, and gone;
Gabriel gives Christ to her, He her to John;
Not fully a mother, she's in orbity;
At once receiver and the legacy.

[continued below]

FROM *"Upon the Annunciation and Passion falling upon one day. 1608"*
All this, and all between, this day hath shown,
Th'abridgement of Christ's story, which makes one
(As in plain maps, the furthest west is east)

Of the angels' *Ave*, and *Consummatum est.*[13]
How well the Church, God's court of faculties,
Deals, in some times, and seldom joining these;
As by the self-fixed pole we never do
Direct our course, but the next star thereto,
Which shows where th'other is, and which we say
(Because it strays not far) doth never stray;
So God by his Church, nearest to him, we know,
And stand firm, if we by her motion go.
His Spirit, as his fiery pillar, doth
Lead, and his Church, as cloud; to one end both:
This Church, by letting these days join, hath shown
Death and conception in mankind is one.
Or 'twas in him the same humility,
That he would be a man, and leave to be:
Or as creation he had made, as God,
With the last judgment, but one period,
His imitating spouse would join in one
Manhood's extremes: he shall come, he is gone:
Or as though one blood drop, which thence did fall,
Accepted, would have served, he yet shed all;
So though the least of his pains, deeds, or words,
Would busy a life, she all this day affords;
This treasure then, in gross, my soul, uplay,[14]
And in my life retail it every day.

---

13 *Ave*—Latin for "hail," the angel Gabriel's greeting to Mary at the Annunciation in Luke 1:28. *Consummatum est*—Latin for "it is finished," the last words of Christ on the cross in John 19:30.

14 *uplay*—archaic for "hoard" (e.g., a reversal of "lay up," as in "but *lay up* for yourselves treasures in heaven," Matthew 6:20).

FROM *"The Call of the Christian"*
JOHN GREENLEAF WHITTIER (American, 1807–1892)

And gently, by a thousand things
  Which o'er our spirits pass,
Like breezes o'er the harp's fine strings,
  Or vapors o'er a glass,
Leaving their token strange and new
  Of music or of shade,
The summons to the right and true
  And merciful is made.

Oh, then, if gleams of truth and light
  Flash o'er thy waiting mind,
Unfolding to thy mental sight
  The wants of human-kind;
If, brooding over human grief,
  The earnest wish is known
To soothe and gladden with relief
  An anguish not thine own;

Though heralded with naught of fear,
  Or outward sign or show;
Though only to the inward ear
  It whispers soft and low;
Though dropping, as the manna fell,
  Unseen, yet from above,
Noiseless as dew-fall, heed it well,—
  Thy Father's call of love!

FROM *The Man Who Was Thursday*

G. K. CHESTERTON (English, 1874–1936)

[Editor's note: Chesterton's rollicking suspense-thriller features a detective plot to infiltrate the Central Council of Anarchists, whose seven members are named for the days of the week (Sunday, Monday, etc.). The main character, Gabriel Syme, finds himself recruited as a spy, first by a regular police officer and then by a mysterious man in a dark room, whose face he never sees. The nature of their conversation takes on apocalyptic overtones that are both wildly funny and profoundly spiritual.]

How can I join you?" asked Syme, with a sort of passion.

"I know for a fact that there is a vacancy at the moment," said the policeman, "as I have the honour to be somewhat in the confidence of the chief of whom I have spoken. You should really come and see him. Or rather, I should not say see him, nobody ever sees him; but you can talk to him if you like."

"Telephone?" inquired Syme, with interest.

"No," said the policeman placidly, "he has a fancy for always sitting in a pitch-dark room. He says it makes his thoughts brighter. Do come along."

Somewhat dazed and considerably excited, Syme allowed himself to be led to a side-door in the long row of buildings of Scotland Yard. Almost before he knew what he was doing, he had been passed through the hands of about four intermediate officials, and was suddenly shown into a room, the abrupt blackness of which startled him like a blaze of light. It was not the ordinary darkness, in which forms can be faintly traced; it was like going suddenly stone-blind.

"Are you the new recruit?" asked a heavy voice.

And in some strange way, though there was not the shadow of a shape in the gloom, Syme knew two things: first, that it came from a man of massive stature; and second, that the man had his back to him.

"Are you the new recruit?" asked the invisible chief, who seemed to have heard all about it. "All right. You are engaged."

Syme, quite swept off his feet, made a feeble fight against this irrevocable phrase.

"I really have no experience," he began.

"No one has any experience," said the other, "of the battle of Armageddon."

"But I am really unfit—"

"You are willing, that is enough," said the unknown.

"Well, really," said Syme, "I don't know of any profession of which mere willingness is the final test."

"I do," said the other—"martyrs. I am condemning you to death. Good day."

Thus it was that when Gabriel Syme came out again into the crimson light of evening, in his shabby black hat and shabby, lawless coat, he came out a member of the New Detective Corps for the frustration of the great conspiracy. Acting under the advice of his friend the policeman (who was professionally inclined to neatness), he trimmed his hair and beard, bought a good hat, clad himself in an exquisite summer suit of light blue-grey, with a pale yellow flower in the button-hole, and, in short, became that elegant and rather insupportable person whom Gregory had first encountered in the little garden of Saffron Park. Before he finally left the police premises his friend provided him with a small blue card, on which was written "The Last Crusade," and a number, the sign of his official authority. He put this carefully in his upper waistcoat pocket, lit a cigarette, and went forth to track and fight the enemy in all the drawing-rooms of London. Where his adventures ultimately led him we have already seen. At about half past one on a February night he found himself steaming in a small tug up the silent Thames, armed with a sword stick and revolver, the duly elected Thursday of the Central Council of Anarchists.

WEEK 18

The Harder Road

OPENING PRAYER

The morning breaks, I place my hand in Thine,
My God, 'tis Thine to lead, to follow mine.

—adapted from the poetry of Gregory of Nazianzus (Cappadocia/modern-day Turkey, AD 325–390)

SCRIPTURES

Psalm 121 | Genesis 12:1–9 | Philippians 3:7–16 | Matthew 7:7–14

READINGS

"Setting Out" by Scott Cairns
"The Pilgrimage" by George Herbert
From *The Divine Comedy: The Inferno* by Dante Alighieri
From *The Pilgrim's Progress* by John Bunyan

PERSONAL PRAYER AND REFLECTION

CLOSING PRAYER

My Lord, I have no clothes to come to thee;
My shoes are pierced and broken with the road;
I am torn and weathered, wounded with the goad.
And soiled with tugging at my weary load:
The more I need thee! A very prodigal
I stagger into thy presence, Lord of me:
One look, my Christ, and at thy feet I fall!
—George MacDonald (Scottish, 1824–1905)

READINGS FOR WEEK 18

Setting Out

SCOTT CAIRNS (American, contemporary)

Pilgrim: What is it that you do here?
Monk: We fall, and we get up again.

In time, even the slowest pilgrim might
articulate a turn. Given time enough,

the slowest pilgrim—even he—might
register some small measure of belated

progress. The road was, more or less, less
compelling than the hut, but as the benefit

of time allowed the hut's distractions to attain
a vaguely musty scent, and all the novel

knickknacks to acquire a fine veneer of bone-
white dust, the road became then somewhat more

attractive, and as the weather made a timely
if quite brief concession, the pilgrim took this all

to be an open invitation to set out.

The Pilgrimage

George Herbert (English, 1593–1633)

I traveled on, seeing the hill, where lay
My expectation.
A long it was and weary way.
The gloomy cave of Desperation
I left on the one, and on the other side
The rock of Pride.

And so I came to Fancy's meadow strowed[15]
With many a flower:
Fain would I here have made abode,
But I was quickened by my hour.
So to Care's copse I came, and there got through
With much ado.

That led me to the wild of Passion, which
Some call the wold;[16]
A wasted place, but sometimes rich.
Here I was robbed of all my gold,
Save one good Angel, which a friend had tied
Close to my side.

At length I got unto the gladsome hill,
Where lay my hope,
Where lay my heart; and climbing still,
When I had gained the brow and top,
A lake of brackish waters on the ground
Was all I found.

With that abashed and struck with many a sting
Of swarming fears,

---

15 *strowed*—archaic for "strewn."

16 *wold*—a wild moor or highland.

I fell and cried, Alas my King!
Can both the way and end be tears?
Yet taking heart I rose, and then perceived
I was deceived:

My hill was further: so I flung away,
Yet heard a cry
Just as I went, *None goes that way*
And lives: If that be all, said I,
After so foul a journey death is fair,
And but a chair.

FROM *The Divine Comedy: The Inferno, Canto III*

DANTE ALIGHIERI (Italian, 1265–1321)

"Through me the way is to the city dolent;[17]
Through me the way is to eternal dole;
Through me the way among the people lost.
Justice incited my sublime Creator;
Created me divine Omnipotence,
The highest Wisdom and the primal Love.
Before me there were no created things,
Only eterne,[18] and I eternal last.
All hope abandon, ye who enter in!"
These words in somber color I beheld
Written upon the summit of a gate;
Whence I: "Their sense is, Master, hard to me!"
And he to me, as one experienced:
"Here all suspicion needs must be abandoned,
All cowardice must needs be here extinct.

17 *dolent*—sorrowful.

18 *eterne*—shorthand for "eternity."

We to the place have come, where I have told thee
Thou shalt behold the people dolorous
Who have foregone the good of intellect."
And after he had laid his hand on mine
With joyful mien, whence I was comforted,
He led me in among the secret things.

FROM *The Pilgrim's Progress*

JOHN BUNYAN (English, 1628–1688)

[Editor's note: Bunyan's classic allegory of Christian's journey to the heavenly city is full of encounters with those who would try to sway Christian from his goal, including his own family, neighbors, and characters like Mr. Worldly Wiseman. But despite occasional detours Christian returns to his course and arrives at a gate that leads to a narrow path—a hard road based on Jesus' words in Matthew 7:13–14.]

Then did Christian address himself to go back; and Evangelist, after he had kissed him, gave him one smile, and bid him God speed. So he went on with haste, neither spake he to any man by the way; nor if any asked him, would he vouchsafe them an answer. He went like one that was all the while treading on forbidden ground, and could by no means think himself safe, till again he was got into the way which he had left to follow Mr. Worldly Wiseman's counsel. So, in process of time, Christian got up to the gate.

Now, over the gate there was written, "Knock, and it shall be opened unto you."

He knocked, therefore, more than once or twice, saying,

"May I now enter here? Will he within
Open to sorry me, though I have been

An undeserving rebel? Then shall I
Not fail to sing his lasting praise on high."

At last there came a grave person to the gate, named Goodwill, who asked who was there, and whence he came, and what he would have.

CHRISTIAN: Here is a poor burdened sinner. I come from the city of Destruction, but am going to Mount Zion, that I may be delivered from the wrath to come; I would therefore, sir, since I am informed that by this gate is the way thither, know if you are willing to let me in.

GOODWILL: I am willing with all my heart, said he; and with that he opened the gate.

So when Christian was stepping in, the other gave him a pull. Then said Christian, What means that? The other told him, A little distance from this gate there is erected a strong castle, of which Beelzebub is the captain: from thence both he and they that are with him, shoot arrows at those that come up to this gate, if haply they may die before they can enter in. Then said Christian, I rejoice and tremble. So when he was got in, the man of the Gate asked him who directed him thither.

CHRISTIAN: Evangelist bid me come hither and knock, as I did: and he said, that you, sir, would tell me what I must do.

GOODWILL: An open door is set before thee, and no man can shut it.

CHRISTIAN: Now I begin to reap the benefits of my hazards.

GOODWILL: But how is it that you came alone?

CHRISTIAN: Because none of my neighbors saw their danger as I saw mine.

GOODWILL: Did any of them know of your coming?

CHRISTIAN: Yes, my wife and children saw me at the first, and called after me to turn again: also, some of my neighbors stood crying and calling after me to return; but I put my fingers in my ears, and so came on my way. . . . But now I am come, such a one as I am, more fit indeed for death by that mountain, than thus to stand talking with my Lord. But O, what a favor is this to me, that yet I am admitted entrance here!

GOODWILL: We make no objections against any, notwithstanding all that they have done before they come hither; they in no wise are cast out. And therefore good Christian, come a little way with me, and I will teach thee about the way thou must go. Look before thee; dost thou see this narrow way? That is the way thou must go. It was cast up by the patriarchs, prophets, Christ, and his apostles, and it is as straight as a rule can make it; this is the way thou must go.

CHRISTIAN: But, are there no turnings nor windings, by which a stranger may lose his way?

GOODWILL: Yes, there are many ways but down upon this, and they are crooked and wide: but thus thou mayest distinguish the right from the wrong, the right only being straight and narrow.

WEEK 19

Put to the Test

OPENING PRAYER

For us,—whatever's undergone,
Thou knowest, willest what is done,
Grief may be joy misunderstood;
Only the Good discerns the good.
I trust Thee while my days go on.
—Elizabeth Barrett Browning
(English, 1806–1861)

SCRIPTURES

Psalm 13 | Genesis 22:1–14 | Hebrews 10:32–39 | Mark 5:21–34

READINGS

"The foolishness of God" by Luci Shaw
"When I consider how my light is spent" by John Milton
"Reflections on 'A Certain Woman'" by Enuma Okoro
"Later Life: A Double Sonnet of Sonnets (XI)" by Christina Rossetti
From "The Wreck of the Deutschland" by Gerard Manley Hopkins

PERSONAL PRAYER AND REFLECTION

CLOSING PRAYER

Whatever's lost, it first was won;
We will not struggle nor impugn.
Perhaps the cup was broken here,

That Heaven's new wine might show more clear.
I praise Thee while my days go on.
—Elizabeth Barrett Browning
(English, 1806-1861)

READINGS FOR WEEK 19

The foolishness of God
1 Corinthians 1:20–25

Luci Shaw (naturalized U.S. citizen, contemporary)

Perform impossibilities
or perish. Thrust out now
the unseasonal ripe figs
among your leaves. Expect
the mountain to be moved.
Hate parents, friends and all
materiality. Love every enemy.
Forgive more times than seventy-
seven. Camel-like, squeeze by
into the kingdom through
the needle's eye. All fear quell.
Hack off your hand, or else
unbloodied, go to hell.

Thus the divine unreason.
Despairing now, you cry
with earthy logic—How?
And I, your God, reply:
Leap from your weedy shallows.
Dive into the moving water.
Eyeless, learn to see

truly. Find in my folly your
true sanity. Then Spirit-driven,
run on my narrow way, sure
as a child. Probe, hold
my unhealed hand, and
bloody, enter heaven.

When I consider how my light is spent

JOHN MILTON (English, 1608–1674)

When I consider how my light is spent
  Ere half my days, in this dark world and wide,
  And that one talent which is death to hide,
  Lodged with me useless, though my soul more bent
To serve therewith my Maker, and present
  My true account, lest he returning chide;
  "Doth God exact day-labor, light denied?"
  I fondly ask; but Patience to prevent
That murmur, soon replies, "God doth not need
  Either man's work or his own gifts; who best
  Bear his mild yoke, they serve him best. His state
Is kingly. Thousands at his bidding speed
  And post o'er land and ocean without rest;
  They also serve who only stand and wait."

Reflections on "A Certain Woman"

ENUMA OKORO (Nigerian-American, contemporary)

1.

I confess to stealing
healings caught on rims
of rough cotton linens.
Securing double blessings
in grief and desperation.
A master turned to claim
His own, to seal my blood flow
for a later date and
I'm lauded for a faith
that bore no options.

2.

If I believed like She did
and pressed through my crowded thoughts
to steal healings and blessings
in desperate faith
fear and trembling kneeling
to confess my theft and my plagues . . .
Would my blood flow stop
as I often fear it may?

Later Life: A Double Sonnet of Sonnets (XI)

CHRISTINA ROSSETTI (English, 1830–1894)

Lifelong our stumbles, lifelong our regret,
    Lifelong our efforts failing and renewed,

While lifelong is our witness, "God is good:"
Who bore with us till now, bears with us yet,
Who still remembers and will not forget,
Who gives us light and warmth and daily food;
And gracious promises half understood,
And glories half unveiled, whereon to set
Our heart of hearts and eyes of our desire;
Uplifting us to longing and to love,
Luring us upward from this world of mire,
Urging us to press on and mount above
Ourselves and all we have had experience of,
Mounting to Him in love's perpetual fire.

FROM *"The Wreck of the Deutschland"*
GERARD MANLEY HOPKINS (English, 1844–1889)

to the happy memory of five Franciscan nuns,
exiles by the Falk Laws, drowned between
midnight and morning of Dec. 7 [1875] . . .

I am soft sift
In an hourglass—at the wall
Fast, but mined with a motion, a drift,
And it crowds and it combs to the fall;
I steady as a water in a well, to a poise, to a pane,
But roped with, always, all the way down from the tall
Fells or flanks of the voel, a vein
Of the gospel proffer, a pressure, a principle, Christ's gift.

I kiss my hand
To the stars, lovely-asunder
Starlight, wafting him out of it; and
Glow, glory in thunder;
Kiss my hand to the dappled-with-damson west:
Since, though he is under the world's splendor and wonder,
His mystery must be instressed, stressed;
For I greet him the days I meet him, and bless when I understand.

Not out of his bliss
Springs the stress felt
Nor first from heaven (and few know this)
Swings the stroke dealt—
Stroke and a stress that stars and storms deliver,
That guilt is hushed by, hearts are flushed by and melt—
But it rides time like riding a river
(And here the faithful waver, the faithless fable and miss).

[continued below]

FROM *"The Wreck of the Deutschland"*

. . . It dates from day
Of his going in Galilee;
Warm-laid grave of a womb-life grey;
Manger, maiden's knee;
The dense and the driven Passion, and frightful sweat;
Thence the discharge of it, there its swelling to be,
Though felt before, though in high flood yet—
What none would have known of it, only the heart, being hard at bay,

Is out with it! Oh,
We lash with the best or worst
Word last! How a lush-kept plush-capped sloe
Will, mouthed to flesh-burst,
Gush!—flush the man, the being with it, sour or sweet,
Brim, in a flash, full!—Hither then, last or first,
To hero of Calvary, Christ,'s feet—
Never ask if meaning it, wanting it, warned of it—men go.

Be adored among men,
God, three-numberèd form;
Wring thy rebel, dogged in den,
Man's malice, with wrecking and storm.
Beyond saying sweet, past telling of tongue,
Thou art lightning and love, I found it, a winter and warm;
Father and fondler of heart thou hast wrung:
Hast thy dark descending and most art merciful then.

With an anvil-ding
And with fire in him forge thy will
Or rather, rather then, stealing as Spring
Through him, melt him but master him still:
Whether at once, as once at a crash Paul,
Or as Austin, a lingering-out sweet skill,
Make mercy in all of us, out of us all
Mastery, but be adored, but be adored King.

WEEK 20

Growing Good

OPENING PRAYER

How good Thou art, O God! All is done for us by Thee, who dost but ask us to give our wills to Thee that we may be pliable as wax in Thy hands.

—Teresa of Avila (Spanish, 1515–1582)

SCRIPTURES

Psalm 101 | Proverbs 3:1–12 | Romans 5:1–5 | Matthew 5:1–16

READINGS

"Called to Be Saints" by Christina Rossetti
From "All Saints' Day" by John Keble
From "In Honor of St. Teresa" by Richard Crashaw
From the Prologue of *Middlemarch* by George Eliot
From the Epilogue of *Middlemarch*

PERSONAL PRAYER AND REFLECTION

CLOSING PRAYER

Alas, O Lord, to what a state dost Thou bring those who love Thee! Yet these sufferings are as nothing compared with the reward Thou wilt give for them. It is right that great riches should be dearly bought.

—Teresa of Avila (Spanish, 1515–1582)

READINGS FOR WEEK 20

Called to Be Saints
CHRISTINA ROSSETTI (English, 1830–1894)

The lowest place. Ah, Lord, how steep and high
  That lowest place whereon a saint shall sit!
Which of us halting, trembling, pressing nigh,
  Shall quite attain to it?

Yet, Lord, Thou pressest nigh to hail and grace
  Some happy soul, it may be still unfit
For Right Hand or for Left Hand, but whose place
  Waits there prepared for it.

FROM *"All Saints' Day"*
JOHN KEBLE (English, 1792–1866)

Think ye the spires that glow so bright
    In front of yonder setting sun,
  Stand by their own unshaken might?
    No—where th' upholding grace is won,
  We dare not ask, nor Heaven would tell,
  But sure from many a hidden dell,
  From many a rural nook unthought of there,
Rises for that proud world the saints' prevailing prayer.

  On, Champions blest, in Jesus' name,
    Short be your strife, your triumph full,

Till every heart have caught your flame,
And, lightened of the world's misrule,
Ye soar those elder saints to meet
Gathered long since at Jesus' feet,
No world of passions to destroy,
Your prayers and struggles o'er, your task all praise and joy.

FROM *"In Honor of St. Teresa"*
RICHARD CRASHAW (English, 1613–1649)

Love, thou art absolute sole Lord
Of life and death. To prove the word,
We'll now appeal to none of all
Those thy old soldiers, great and tall
Ripe men of martyrdom, that could reach down
With strong arms, their triumphant crown;
Such as could with lusty breath
Speak loud into the face of death
Their great Lord's glorious name, to none
Of those whose spacious bosoms spread a throne
For Love at large to fill: spare blood and sweat;
And see him take a private seat,
Making his mansion in the mild
And milky soul of a soft child.
Scarce has she learned to lisp the name
Of martyr; yet she thinks it shame
Life should so long play with that breath
Which spent can buy so brave a death.
She never undertook to know
What death with love should have to do;

Nor has she ever yet understood
Why to show love, she should shed blood
Yet though she cannot tell you why
She can love, and she can die.

From the Prologue of *Middlemarch*

George Eliot (a.k.a. Mary Ann Evans; English, 1819–1880)

[Editor's note: Eliot begins her masterpiece by casting the main character, Dorothea Brooke, as a modern-day Teresa of Avila, who aspired to accomplish great things for God but lived mostly in obscurity. Dorothea (as described in the reading from week 3), in a fit of piety, first marries a much older clergyman—a decision that some find baffling. When the Reverend Casaubon dies, she marries his much younger cousin, whom she really loves, but which is yet another unwise choice in the eyes of her community. By the epilogue, however, Eliot has developed a woman whose life may not have been what she wanted but which nonetheless gave her a quiet fidelity and strength.]

That Spanish woman who lived three hundred years ago was certainly not the last of her kind. Many Theresas have been born who found for themselves no epic life wherein there was a constant unfolding of far-resonant action; perhaps only a life of mistakes, the offspring of a certain spiritual grandeur ill-matched with the meanness of opportunity; perhaps a tragic failure which found no sacred poet and sank unwept into oblivion. With dim lights and tangled circumstance they tried to shape their thought and deed in noble agreement; but after all, to common eyes their struggles seemed mere inconsistency and formlessness; for these later-born Theresas were helped by no coherent social faith and order which could perform the function of knowledge for the ardently willing soul. Their ardor alternated between a vague ideal and the common yearning of womanhood; so that the one was disapproved as extravagance, and the other condemned as a lapse.

Some have felt that these blundering lives are due to the inconvenient indefiniteness with which the Supreme Power has fashioned the natures of women: if there were one level of feminine incompetence as strict as the ability to count three and no more, the social lot of women might be treated with scientific certitude. Meanwhile the indefiniteness remains, and the limits of variation are really much wider than any one would imagine from the sameness of women's coiffure and the favorite love-stories in prose and verse. Here and there a cygnet is reared uneasily among the ducklings in the brown pond, and never finds the living stream in fellowship with its own oary-footed kind. Here and there is born a Saint Theresa, foundress of nothing, whose loving heart-beats and sobs after an unattained goodness tremble off and are dispersed among hindrances, instead of centering in some long-recognizable deed.

FROM the Epilogue of *Middlemarch*

Sir James never ceased to regard Dorothea's second marriage as a mistake; and indeed this remained the tradition concerning it in Middlemarch, where she was spoken of to a younger generation as a fine girl who married a sickly clergyman, old enough to be her father, and in little more than a year after his death gave up her estate to marry his cousin—young enough to have been his son, with no property, and not well-born. Those who had not seen anything of Dorothea usually observed that she could not have been "a nice woman," else she would not have married either the one or the other.

Certainly those determining acts of her life were not ideally beautiful. They were the mixed result of a young and noble impulse struggling amidst the conditions of an imperfect social state, in which great feelings will often take the aspect of error, and great faith the aspect of illusion. For there is no creature whose inward being is so strong that it is not greatly determined by what lies outside it. A new Theresa will hardly have the opportunity of reforming a conventual[19] life, any more than a new Antigone will spend her heroic piety in daring all for the sake of a brother's burial: the medium in which their ardent deeds took shape is for ever gone. But we insignificant people with our daily words and acts are preparing the lives of many Dorotheas, some of which may present a far sadder sacrifice than that of the Dorothea whose story we know.

Her finely-touched spirit had still its fine issues, though they were not widely visible. Her full nature, like that river of which Cyrus broke the strength, spent itself in channels which had no great name on the earth. But the effect of her being on those around her was incalculably diffusive: for the growing good of the world is partly dependent on unhistoric acts; and that things are not so ill with you and me as they might have been, is half owing to the number who lived faithfully a hidden life, and rest in unvisited tombs.

19 *conventual*—having to do with a convent or religious order.

WEEK 21

Communion of the Body

OPENING PRAYER

We feel and see with different hearts and eyes:—
Ah Christ, if all our hearts could meet in Thee
How well it were for them and well for me,
Our hearts Thy dear accepted sacrifice.
—CHRISTINA ROSSETTI (English, 1830–1894)

SCRIPTURES

PSALM 133 | GENESIS 33:1–11 | EPHESIANS 4:1–16 | MATTHEW 18:15–35

READINGS

"Disciplinary Treatises: (4) The Communion of the Body" by SCOTT CAIRNS
From "St. Andrew's Day" by JOHN KEBLE
"A General Communion" by ALICE MEYNELL
"As kingfishers catch fire, dragonflies draw flame" by GERARD MANLEY HOPKINS
From "The Rime of the Ancient Mariner (Part VII)" by SAMUEL TAYLOR COLERIDGE

PERSONAL PRAYER AND REFLECTION

CLOSING PRAYER

Be praised, my Lord, through those who forgive for love of you; through those who endure sickness and trial.

Happy those who endure in peace,
for by you, Most High, they will be crowned.
—Francis of Assisi (Italian, ca. 1181–1226)

READINGS FOR WEEK 21

Disciplinary Treatises: (4) The Communion of the Body

Scott Cairns (American, contemporary)

The Christ in his own heart is weaker
than the Christ in the word of his brother.
—Bonhoeffer

Scattered, petulant, argumentative,
the diverse members generally find
little, nothing of their own, to offer

one another. Like us all, the saved
need saving mostly from themselves, and so
they make progress, if at all, by dying

to what they can, acquiescing to this
new pressure, new wind, new breath that would fill
them with something better than their own

good intentions. Or schemes of community.
Or their few articulate innovations
in dogma. What the Ghost expects of them

is a purer than customary will
to speak together, a *mere* willingness
to hear expressed in the fragmentary

figures of one another's speech the mute
and palpable identity they share,
scoured clear of impediment and glare,

the uncanny evidence that here
in the stillest air between them the One
we call the Ghost insinuates his care

for the unexpected word now fondling
the tongue, now falling here, incredible
confession—that they would be believers,

who startle to suspect among the scraps
of Babel's gritty artifacts one stone,
irreducible fossil, capable

of bearing love's unprovoked inscription
in the locus of its term.

From "St. Andrew's Day"

JOHN KEBLE (English, 1792–1866)

He first findeth his own brother Simon, and saith unto him, We have found the Messiah. . . . And he brought him to Jesus.

St. John 1:41–42

When brothers part for manhood's race,
  What gift may most endearing prove
To keep fond memory in her place,
  And certify a brother's love?

'Tis true, bright hours together told,
  And blissful dreams in secret shared,
Serene or solemn, gay or bold,
  Shall last in fancy unimpaired.

E'en round the death-bed of the good
  Such dear remembrances will hover,
And haunt us with no vexing mood
  When all the cares of earth are over.

But yet our craving spirits feel,
  We shall live on, though Fancy die,
And seek a surer pledge—a seal
  Of love to last eternally.

Who art thou, that wouldst grave thy name
  Thus deeply in a brother's heart?
Look on this saint, and learn to frame
  Thy love-charm with true Christian art.

First seek thy Savior out, and dwell
  Beneath this shadow of His roof,
Till thou have scanned His features well,
  And known Him for the Christ by proof;

Such proof as they are sure to find
  Who spend with Him their happy days,
Clean hands, and a self-ruling mind
  Ever in tune for love and praise.

Then, potent with the spell of Heaven,
  Go, and thine erring brother gain,
Entice him home to be forgiven,
  Till he, too, see his Savior plain.

Or, if before thee in the race,
  Urge him with thine advancing tread,
Till, like twin stars, with even pace,
  Each lucid course be duly aped.

No fading frail memorial give
To soothe his soul when thou art gone,
But wreaths of hope for aye to live,
And thoughts of good together done.

That so, before the judgment-seat,
Though changed and glorified each face,
Not unremembered ye may meet
For endless ages to embrace.

A General Communion

ALICE MEYNELL (English, 1847–1922)

I saw the throng, so deeply separate,
Fed at one only board—
The devout people, moved, intent, elate,
And the devoted Lord.

Oh struck apart! not side from human side,
But soul from human soul,
As each asunder absorbed the multiplied,
The ever unparted whole.

I saw this people as a field of flowers,
Each grown at such a price
The sum of unimaginable powers
Did no more than suffice.

A thousand single central daisies they,
A thousand of the one;
For each, the entire monopoly of day;
For each, the whole of the devoted sun.

As kingfishers catch fire, dragonflies draw flame
GERARD MANLEY HOPKINS (English, 1844–1889)

As kingfishers catch fire, dragonflies draw flame;
  As tumbled over rim in roundy wells
  Stones ring; like each tucked string tells, each hung bell's
Bow swung finds tongue to fling out broad its name;
Each mortal thing does one thing and the same:
  Deals out that being indoors each one dwells;
  Selves—goes its self; *myself* it speaks and spells,
Crying *What I do is me: for that I came.*

I say more: the just man justices;
  Keeps grace: that keeps all his goings graces;
Acts in God's eye what in God's eye he is—
  Christ. For Christ plays in ten thousand places,
Lovely in limbs, and lovely in eyes not his
  To the Father through the features of men's faces.

From "The Rime of the Ancient Mariner (Part VII)"
SAMUEL TAYLOR COLERIDGE (English, 1772–1834)

[Editor's note: A young man on his way to a wedding is accosted by an ancient mariner, who forces him to hear his tale. The old man tells of how, in a moment of thoughtless cruelty, he killed an albatross that had been accompanying his ship's crew at sea—and the horrors that ensued: the hanging of the albatross around his neck; the death of all the crew but himself; the possession of the dead crew by spirits which sailed the ship through a hell-like sea; and the arrival of the death-ship upon a shore. There the mariner, more dead than alive, is rescued by a Hermit and several others before the death-ship sinks in the bay;

and his appearance strikes fear into the hearts of his rescuers. The epic poem concludes with an appeal to Christian community: indeed, the gravest consequence of the mariner's sin was not the guilt of killing a creature but being cut off from fellowship with humanity.]

"O shrieve me, shrieve me, holy man!"
The Hermit crossed his brow.
"Say quick," quoth he, "I bid thee say—
What manner of man art thou?"

Forthwith this frame of mine was wrenched
With a woeful agony,
Which forced me to begin my tale;
And then it left me free.

Since then, at an uncertain hour,
That agony returns:
And till my ghastly tale is told,
This heart within me burns.

I pass, like night, from land to land;
I have strange power of speech;
That moment that his face I see,
I know the man that must hear me:
To him my tale I teach.

What loud uproar bursts from that door!
The wedding-guests are there:
But in the garden-bower the bride
And bride-maids singing are:
And hark the little vesper bell,
Which biddeth me to prayer!

O Wedding-Guest! this soul hath been
Alone on a wide wide sea:
So lonely 'twas, that God himself

Scarce seemèd there to be.

O sweeter than the marriage-feast,
'Tis sweeter far to me,
To walk together to the kirk
With a goodly company!—

To walk together to the kirk,
And all together pray,
While each to his great Father bends,
Old men, and babes, and loving friends
And youths and maidens gay!

Farewell, farewell! but this I tell
To thee, thou Wedding-Guest!
He prayeth well, who loveth well
Both man and bird and beast.

He prayeth best, who loveth best
All things both great and small;
For the dear God who loveth us,
He made and loveth all.

WEEK 22

Cloud of Witnesses

OPENING PRAYER

Betray, kind husband, thy spouse to our sights,
And let mine amorous soul court thy mild dove,
Who is most true and pleasing to thee then
When she is embraced and open to most men.
—JOHN DONNE (English, 1572–1631)

SCRIPTURES

PSALM 150 | 1 KINGS 8:54–66 | HEBREWS 11:32–12:2 | JOHN 15:1–17

READINGS

"Little Girls in Church (II)" by KATHLEEN NORRIS
"Faith of Our Fathers" by PAUL J. WILLIS
From "St. Mark's Day" by JOHN KEBLE
From *Lake Wobegon Days* by GARRISON KEILLOR

PERSONAL PRAYER AND REFLECTION

CLOSING PRAYER

Lord of this erring flock!
Thou whose soft showers distil
On ocean waste or rock,
Free as on Hermon hill,
Do Thou our craven spirits cheer,
And shame away the selfish tear.
—JOHN KEBLE (English, 1792–1866)

READINGS FOR WEEK 22

Little Girls in Church (II)

KATHLEEN NORRIS (American, contemporary)

I worry for the girls.
I once had braids,
and wore lace that made me suffer.
I had not yet done the things
that would need forgiving.

Church was for singing, and so I sang.
I received a Bible, stars
for all the verses;
I turned and ran.

The music brought me back
from time to time,
singing hymns
in the great breathing body
of a congregation.
And once in Paris, as
I stepped into Notre Dame
to get out of the rain,
the organist began to play:
I stood rooted to the spot,
looked up, and believed.

It didn't last.
Dear girls, my friends,
may you find great love
within you, starlike
and wild, as wide as grass,

solemn as the moon.
I will pray for you, if I can.

Faith of Our Fathers
PAUL J. WILLIS (American, contemporary)

The faculty ate lunch and sang today,
a dark day in the old chapel. We lent
our less than thousand tongues

unto a fortress mighty as it's ever been,
and though there were brave women too
we bellowed like bass organ pipes,

joining mostly our forefathers
in echoes of their hallowing,
our brief and particular stanza.

So many rich voices among us,
grave and deep and reverberant,
and this was a great comfort to me—

to be still a child after all, still surrounded
by grown men growling low
in their unmistakable harmony.

From "St. Mark's Day"

John Keble (English, 1792–1866)

> *And the contention was so sharp between them, that they departed asunder one from the other. Acts xv. 30. Compare 2 Tim. iv. 11. Take Mark, and bring him with thee: for he is profitable to me for the ministry.*

Oh! who shall dare in this frail scene
On holiest happiest thoughts to lean,
  On Friendship, Kindred, or on Love?
Since not Apostles' hands can clasp
Each other in so firm a grasp
  But they shall change and variance prove.

Yet deem not, on such parting sad
Shall dawn no welcome dear and glad:
  Divided in their earthly race,
Together at the glorious goal,
Each leading many a rescued soul,
  The faithful champions shall embrace. . . .

And sometimes e'en beneath the moon
The Savior gives a gracious boon,
  When reconciled Christians meet,
And face to face, and heart to heart,
High thoughts of holy love impart
  In silence meek, or converse sweet.

Companion of the Saints! 'twas thine
To taste that drop of peace divine,
  When the great soldier of thy Lord
Called thee to take his last farewell,
Teaching the Church with joy to tell
  The story of your love restored.

O then the glory and the bliss,
When all that pained or seemed amiss
  Shall melt with earth and sin away!
When saints beneath their Savior's eye,
Filled with each other's company,
  Shall spend in love the eternal day!

FROM *Lake Wobegon Days*

GARRISON KEILLOR (American, contemporary)

[Editor's note: Keillor's fictitious small town of Lake Wobegon has become iconic of American midwestern experience, including its myopic, if mostly harmless, prejudices between Protestants and Catholics. In describing the narrator's childhood faith community, Keillor manages to capture both the intimacy of the community and the hardening of prejudice toward those outside of it—even if the outsiders are in fact one's brothers and sisters in faith.]

We were Sanctified Brethren, a sect so tiny that nobody but us and God knew about it, so when kids asked what I was, I just said Protestant. It was too much to explain, like having six toes. You would rather keep your shoes on.

Grandpa Cotton was once tempted toward Lutheranism by a preacher who gave a rousing sermon on grace that Grandpa heard as a young man while taking Aunt Esther's dog home who had chased a Model T across town. He sat down on the church steps and listened to the voice boom out the open windows until he made up his mind to go in and unite with the truth, but he took one look from the vestibule and left. "He was dressed up like the Pope of Rome," said Grandpa, "and the altar and the paintings and the gold candlesticks—my gosh, it was just a big show. And he was reading the whole darn thing off a page, like an actor."

Jesus said, "Where two or three are gathered together in my name, there am I in the midst of them," and the Brethren believed that was enough. We met in Uncle Al's and Aunt Flo's bare living room with plain folding chairs arranged facing in toward the middle. No clergyman in a block smock. No organ or piano, for that would make one person too prominent. No upholstery, it would lead to complacency. No picture of Jesus, He was in our hearts. The faithful sat down at the appointed hour and waited for the Spirit to move one of them to speak or to pray or to give out a hymn from our Little Flock hymnal. No musical notation, for music must come from the heart and not off a page. We sang the texts to a tune that fit the meter, of the many tunes we all knew. The idea of reading a prayer was sacrilege to us—"if a man can't remember what he wants to say to God, let him sit down and think a little harder," Grandpa said.

"There's the Lord's Prayer," said Aunt Esther meekly. We were sitting on the porch after Sunday dinner. Esther and Harvey were visiting from Minneapolis and had attended Lake Wobegon Lutheran, she having turned Lutheran when she married him, a subject that was never brought up in our family.

"You call that prayer? Sitting and reciting like a bunch of schoolchildren?"

Harvey cleared his throat and turned to me with a weak smile. "Speaking of school, how are you doing?" he asked.

There was a lovely silence in the Brethren assembled on Sunday morning as we waited for the Spirit. Either the Spirit was moving someone to speak who was taking his sweet time or else the Spirit was playing a wonderful joke on us and letting us sit, or perhaps silence was the point of it. We sat listening to rain on the roof, distant traffic, a radio playing from across the street, kids whizzing by on bikes, dogs barking, as we waited for the Spirit to inspire us. It was like sitting on the porch with your family, when nobody feels that they have to make talk. So quiet in church. Minutes drifted by in silence that was sweet to us. The old Regulator clock ticked, the rain stopped and the room changed light as the sun broke through—shafts of brilliant sun through the windows and motes of dust falling through it—the smell of clean clothes and floor wax and wine and the fresh bread of Aunt Flo which was Christ's body given for us. Jesus in our midst, who loved us. So peaceful, and we loved each other too. I thought perhaps the Spirit was leading me to say that, but I was just a boy, and children were supposed to keep still. And my affections were not pure. They were tainted with a sneaking admiration of Catholics—Catholic Christmas, Easter, the Living Rosary, and the Blessing of the Animals, all magnificent. Everything we did was plain, but they were regal and gorgeous—especially the Feast Day of St. Francis, which they did right out in the open, a feast for the eyes. Cows, horses, some pigs, right on the church lawn. The turmoil, animals bellowing and barking and clucking and cats scheming how to escape and suddenly leaping out of the girl's arms who was holding on tight, the cat dashing through the crowd, dogs straining at the leash, and the ocarina band of third-graders playing Catholic dirges, and the great calm of the sisters, and the flags, and the Knights of Columbus decked out in their handsome black suits—I stared at it until my eyes almost fell out, and then I wished it would go on much longer.

"Christians," my uncle Al used to say, "do not go in for show," referring to the Catholics. We were sanctified by the blood of the Lord, therefore we were saints, like St. Francis, but we didn't go in for feasts or ceremonies, involving animals or not. We went in for sitting, all nineteen of us, in Uncle Al's and Aunt Flo's living room on Sunday morning and having a plain meeting and singing hymns in our poor thin voices while not far away the Catholics were whooping it up. I wasn't allowed inside Our Lady, of course, but if the Blessing of the Animals on the Feast Day of St. Francis was any indication, Lord, I didn't know but what they had elephants in there and acrobats. I sat in our little group and envied them for the splendor and gorgeousness, as we tried to sing without even a harmonica to give us the pitch. Hymns, Uncle Al said, didn't have to be sung perfect, because God looks on the heart, and if you are In The Spirit, then all praise is good.

WEEK 23

In God's House

OPENING PRAYER

Thy saints are comforted, I know,
  And love Thy house of prayer;
I therefore go where others go,
  But find no comfort there.

Oh make this heart rejoice, or ache;
  Decide this doubt for me;
And if it be not broken, break,
  And heal it, if it be.
—WILLIAM COWPER (English, 1731–1800)

SCRIPTURES

PSALM 122 | 2 CHRONICLES 7:1–10 | ACTS 2:43–47 | LUKE 18:9–14

READINGS

"The Windows" by GEORGE HERBERT
"Bethany Chapel" by LUCI SHAW
"Cathedral Windows" by MARY F. C. PRATT
From *Mansfield Park* by JANE AUSTEN

PERSONAL PRAYER AND REFLECTION

CLOSING PRAYER

And whilst this universal choir,
That Church in triumph, this in warfare here,
Warmed with one all-partaking fire

Of love, that none be lost, which cost thee dear,
Prays ceaselessly, and thou hearken too
(Since to be gracious
Our task is treble: to pray, bear, and do)
Hear this prayer, Lord; O Lord, deliver us
From trusting in those prayers though poured out thus.
—JOHN DONNE (English, 1572–1631)

READINGS FOR WEEK 23

The Windows

GEORGE HERBERT (English, 1593–1633)

Lord, how can man preach thy eternal word?
He is a brittle crazy glass:
Yet in thy temple thou dost him afford
This glorious and transcendent place,
To be a window, through thy grace.

But when thou dost anneal[20] in glass thy story,
Making thy life to shine within
The holy Preacher's; then the light and glory
More reverend grows, and more doth win:
Which else shows waterish, bleak, and thin.

Doctrine and life, colors and light, in one
When they combine and mingle, bring
A strong regard and awe: but speech alone
Doth vanish like a flaring thing;
And in the ear, not conscience ring.

20 *anneal*—to heat and then cool in order to strengthen or temper.

Bethany Chapel

Luci Shaw (naturalized U.S. citizen, contemporary)

Bracketed between the first
tentative prayers, a silence fills
this place, a shadowed listening
as our separateness seeks out
the Spirit's focus for this hour
and gathers strength enough
to peer and soar
into small, shining arcs of praise
held at their lower ends
by the old hymns. Christ
in this crowd of rest and rising
humbles himself again to our
humanity; and like the sheep
(trembling in the shearer's hands)
surrenders to us once more
in quietness.

As at his dark birth and death
we had his body in our fingers,
now, again, we split the whiteness
of his loaf by turns, and tasting
his imaged life against
the cup's cool rim
we take him in.
Nourished by that final flesh,
that ultimate blood behind
the chosen signs, our God-thoughts,
seeds of worship, multiply to words.
Light flows down to us, and back,
joins us in one body of fire—

one polyphon of light now
sounding out himself—
one flame of singing
burning into being.

Cathedral Windows

MARY F. C. PRATT (American, contemporary)

I take the same walk every morning down a town road
past fields in various stages of decay,
old barns full of junk,
a tilting silo, its rusty hoops barely holding the grey slats together.
I pass long white driveways leading to new houses
built in old woodlots or sugarbushes or pastures.
Now and then something catches me up:
a mother otter swimming circles in a pond
whistling to her capering brood,
a long milksnake basking on the blacktop,
two jade frogs crouching in a ditch—
they squeak and plop into the water when I pass,
leaving hollows in the soft mud like the imprints of fists.
One morning, it was a piece of blue
set in the wall of a barn—
the color of cold winter skies—
blue like the best stained glass,
offerings to Our Lady.
The Virgin Mary's Jewel Box—
Henry Adams' name for the cathedral at Chartres—
was filled to the vaulting with gems;
the darkest corners made beautiful

because that was the way She wanted it.
It was what She liked.
For a heartbeat I believed that someone
had set such a window high in the old wooden wall,
the barn a cathedral!
So, passing on a hot day, one could slip into
that deep blue shade scented with cows and hay,
sit a minute in the stillness, ask a question,
leave a scrap of something—
a fistful of red clover, a pigeon feather—
to seal a promise, keep a vow.
But it was plastic, after all,
a blue tarp stapled there
to keep out the wind and rain.
Once in a magazine, I read about
the restoration of the windows at Chartres.
People were complaining, missing the patina of dirt
that made the glass look like slides on a dark screen
instead of jewels letting in the light.

FROM *Mansfield Park*

JANE AUSTEN (English, 1775–1817)

[Editor's note: A lively party of young people visits the Rushworth country estate to tour the buildings and grounds. Among the party are a sensible future clergyman, Edmund Bertram, his shy but adoring cousin Fanny, and his clever, beautiful admirer Miss Crawford—who, incidentally, is unaware of his future profession. Their subsequent discussion about the role of chapels in communal estate life and the abandoned practice of family prayer highlights the tension many believers feel between duty and passionate faith. Here we are given a rare glimpse of Austen's own views on the subject: that disciplining ourselves to join with others in worship, even when we don't feel like it, somehow changes us.]

Having visited many more rooms than could be supposed to be of any other use than to contribute to the window tax, and find employment for housemaids, "Now," said Mrs. Rushworth, "we are coming to the chapel, which properly we ought to enter from above, and look down upon; but as we are quite among friends, I will take you in this way, if you will excuse me."

They entered. Fanny's imagination had prepared her for something grander than a mere, spacious, oblong room, fitted up for the purpose of devotion—with nothing more striking or more solemn than the profusion of mahogany, and the crimson velvet cushions appearing over the ledge of the family gallery above. "I am disappointed," said she, in a low voice, to Edmund. "This is not my idea of a chapel. There is nothing awful here, nothing melancholy, nothing grand. Here are no aisles, no arches, no inscriptions, no banners. No banners, cousin, to be 'blown by the night wind of Heaven.' No sign that a 'Scottish monarch sleeps below.'"

"You forget, Fanny, how lately all this has been built, and for how confined a purpose, compared with the old chapels of castles and monasteries. It was only for the private use of the family. They have been buried, I suppose, in the parish church. *There* you must look for the banners and the achievements."

"It was foolish of me not to think of all that, but I am disappointed."

Mrs. Rushworth began her relation. "This chapel was fitted up as you see it, in James the Second's time. Before that period, as I understand, the pews were only wainscot; and there is some reason to think that the linings and cushions of the pulpit and family-seat were only purple cloth; but this is not quite certain. It is a handsome chapel, and was formerly in constant use both morning and evening. Prayers were always read in it by the domestic chaplain, within the memory of many. But the late Mr. Rushworth left it off."

"Every generation has its improvements," said Miss Crawford, with a smile, to Edmund.

[continued below]

FROM *Mansfield Park*

Mrs. Rushworth was gone to repeat her lesson to Mr. Crawford; and Edmund, Fanny, and Miss Crawford remained in a cluster together.

"It is a pity," cried Fanny, "that the custom should have been discontinued. It was a valuable part of former times. There is something in a chapel and chaplain so much in character with a great house, with one's ideas of what such a household should be! A whole family assembling regularly for the purpose of prayer, is fine!"

"Very fine indeed!" said Miss Crawford, laughing. "It must do the heads of the family a great deal of good to force all the poor housemaids and footmen to leave business and pleasure, and say their prayers here twice a day, while they are inventing excuses themselves for staying away."

"*That* is hardly Fanny's idea of a family assembling," said Edmund. "If the master and mistress do *not* attend themselves, there must be more harm than good in the custom."

"At any rate, it is safer to leave people to their own devices on such subjects. Everybody likes to go their own way—to choose their own time and manner of devotion. The obligation of attendance, the formality, the restraint, the length of time—altogether it is a formidable thing, and what nobody likes: and if the good people who used to kneel and gape in that gallery could have foreseen that the time would ever come when men and women might lie another ten minutes in bed, when they woke with a headache, without danger of reprobation, because chapel was missed, they would have jumped with joy and envy. Cannot you imagine with what unwilling feelings the former belles of the house of Rushworth did many a time repair to this chapel? The young Mrs. Eleanors and Mrs. Bridgets—starched up into seeming piety, but with heads full of something very different—especially if the poor chaplain were not worth looking at—and, in those days, I fancy parsons were very inferior even to what they are now."

For a few moments she was unanswered. Fanny colored and looked at Edmund, but felt too angry for speech; and *he* needed a little recollection before he could say, "Your lively mind can hardly be serious even on serious subjects. You have given us an amusing sketch, and human nature cannot say it was not so. We must all feel *at times* the difficulty of fixing our thoughts as we could wish; but if you are supposing it a frequent thing, that is to say, a weakness grown into a habit from neglect, what could be expected from the *private* devotions of such persons? Do you think that minds which are suffered, which are indulged in wanderings in a chapel, would be more collected in a closet?"

"Yes, very likely. They would have two chances at least in their favor. There would be less to distract the attention from without, and it would not be tried so long."

"The mind which does not struggle against itself under one circumstance, would find objects to distract in the other, I believe; and the influence of the place and of example may often rouse better feelings than are begun with. The greater length of the service, however, I admit to be sometimes too hard a stretch upon the mind. One wishes it were not so—but I have not yet left Oxford long enough to forget what chapel prayers are."

WEEK 24

It Is Finished

OPENING PRAYER

Be praised, my Lord, through our Sister Bodily Death,
from whose embrace no living person can escape.
Woe to those who die in mortal sin!
Happy those she finds doing your most holy will.
The second death can do no harm to them.
—Francis of Assisi (Italian, ca. 1181–1226)

SCRIPTURES

Psalm 90 | Genesis 49:28–50:14 | Romans 5:12–17 | John 11:1–17

READINGS

"Amen." by Christina Rossetti
"After the Last Kiss" by Scott Cairns
"Consolation" by Elizabeth Barrett Browning
From *The Death of Ivan Ilyich* by Leo Tolstoy

PERSONAL PRAYER AND REFLECTION

CLOSING PRAYER

Though sin and death conspire
To rob thee of thy praise,
Still towards thee I'll aspire,
And thou dull hearts canst raise.
Open thy door;
And when grim death

Shall stop this breath
I'll praise thee more.
—RICHARD BAXTER (English, 1615–1691)

READINGS FOR WEEK 24

Amen.

CHRISTINA ROSSETTI (English, 1830–1894)

It is over. What is over?
Nay, how much is over truly:
Harvest days we toiled to sow for;
Now the sheaves are gathered newly,
Now the wheat is garnered duly.

It is finished. What is finished?
Much is finished known or unknown:
Lives are finished; time diminished;
Was the fallow field left unsown?
Will these buds be always unblown?

It suffices. What suffices?
All suffices reckoned rightly:
Spring shall bloom where now the ice is,
Roses make the bramble sightly,
And the quickening sun shine brightly,
And the latter wind blow lightly,
And my garden teem with spices.

After the Last Kiss

SCOTT CAIRNS (American, contemporary)

By now I'm dead. Make what you will of that.
But granted you are alive, you will need
to be making something more as well. Prayers
have been made, for instance, but (trust me)

the dead are oblivious to such late sessions.
Settle instead for food, common meals of thick soup.
Invite your friends. Make lively conversation
among steaming bowls, lifting heavy spoons.

If there is bread (there really must be bread),
tear it coarsely and hand each guest his share
for intinction in the soup. Something to say?
Say it now. Let the napkins fall and stay.

Kiss each guest when time comes for parting.
They may be embarrassed, caught without wit
or custom. (See them shifting from foot to
foot at the open door?) Could be you will

repeat your farewells a time or two more
than seems fit. But had you not embraced them
at such common departures, prayers will
fall as dry crumbs, nor will they comfort you.

Consolation

ELIZABETH BARRETT BROWNING (English, 1806–1861)

All are not taken; there are left behind
Living Belovèds, tender looks to bring

And make the daylight still a happy thing,
And tender voices, to make soft the wind:
But if it were not so—if I could find
No love in all this world for comforting,
Nor any path but hollowly did ring
Where "dust to dust" the love from life disjoined;
And if, before those sepulchres unmoving
I stood alone (as some forsaken lamb
Goes bleating up the moors in weary dearth)
Crying "Where are ye, O my loved and loving?"—
I know a voice would sound, "Daughter, I AM.
Can I suffice for Heaven and not for earth?"

FROM *The Death of Ivan Ilyich*

LEO TOLSTOY (Russian, 1828–1910)

[Editor's note: As described in the editor's note for week 8, Tolstoy's elegant novella explores the psychology of sin and suffering through the terminally ill Ivan Ilyich. Here Ivan is mere hours from death, forced to face the truth that his has not been a life well lived. But in the end, death does not have the last word.]

From that moment the screaming began that continued for three days, and was so terrible that one could not hear it through two closed doors without horror. At the moment he answered his wife realized that he was lost, that there was no return, that the end had come, the very end, and his doubts were still unsolved and remained doubts.

"Oh! Oh! Oh!" he cried in various intonations. He had begun by screaming "I won't!" and continued screaming on the letter "O."

For three whole days, during which time did not exist for him, he struggled in that black sack into which he was being thrust by an invisible, resistless force. He struggled as a man condemned to death struggles in the hands of the executioner, knowing that he cannot save himself. And every moment he felt that despite all his efforts he was drawing nearer and nearer to what terrified him. He felt that his agony was due to his being thrust into that black hole and still more to his not being able to get right into it. He was hindered from getting into it by his conviction that his life had been a good one. That very justification of his life held him fast and prevented his moving forward, and it caused him most torment of all.

Suddenly some force struck him in the chest and side, making it still harder to breathe, and he fell through the hole and there at the bottom was a light. What had happened to him was like the sensation one sometimes experiences in a railway carriage when one thinks one is going backwards while one is really going forwards and suddenly becomes aware of the real direction.

"Yes, it was not the right thing," he said to himself, "but that's no matter. It can be done. But what is the right thing?" he asked himself, and suddenly grew quiet.

[continued below]

FROM *The Death of Ivan Ilyich*

This occurred at the end of the third day, two hours before his death. Just then his schoolboy son had crept softly in and gone up to the bedside. The dying man was still screaming desperately and waving his arms. His hand fell on the boy's head, and the boy caught it, pressed it to his lips, and began to cry.

At that very moment Ivan Ilyich fell through and caught sight of the light, and it was revealed to him that though his life had not been what it should have been, this could still be rectified. He asked himself, "What is the right thing?" and grew still, listening. Then he felt that someone was kissing his hand. He opened his eyes, looked at his son, and felt sorry for him. His wife came up to him and he glanced at her. She was gazing at him open-mouthed, with undried tears on her nose and cheek and a despairing look on her face. He felt sorry for her too.

"Yes, I am making them wretched," he thought. "They are sorry, but it will be better for them when I die." He wished to say this but had not the strength to utter it. "Besides, why speak? I must act," he thought. With a look at his wife he indicated his son and said: "Take him away . . . sorry for him . . . sorry for you too . . ." He tried to add, "Forgive me," but said "Forego" and waved his hand, knowing that He whose understanding mattered would understand.

And suddenly it grew clear to him that what had been oppressing him and would not leave him was all dropping away at once from two sides, from ten sides, and from all sides. He was sorry for them, he must act so as not to hurt them: release them and free himself from these sufferings.

"How good and how simple!" he thought. "And the pain?" he asked himself. "What has become of it? Where are you, pain?"

He turned his attention to it.

"Yes, here it is. Well, what of it? Let the pain be."

"And death . . . where is it?"

He sought his former accustomed fear of death and did not find it.

"Where is it? What death?" There was no fear because there was no death.

In place of death there was light.

"So that's what it is!" he suddenly exclaimed aloud. "What joy!"

To him all this happened in a single instant, and the meaning of that instant did not change. For those present his agony continued for another two hours. Something rattled in his throat, his emaciated body twitched, then the gasping and rattle became less and less frequent.

"It is finished!" said someone near him.

He heard these words and repeated them in his soul.

"Death is finished," he said to himself. "It is no more!"

He drew in a breath, stopped in the midst of a sigh, stretched out, and died.

WEEK 25

A Better Resurrection

OPENING PRAYER

"Child, get up," You say;
and thus, trembling, we rise,
and follow You. *Amen.*

SCRIPTURES

PSALM 103 | EZEKIEL 37:1–14 | ROMANS 6:1–11 | JOHN 11:18–44

READINGS

"A Better Resurrection" by CHRISTINA ROSSETTI
"The Caged Skylark" by GERARD MANLEY HOPKINS
"Resurrection" by JOHN DONNE
From *Peace Like a River* by LEIF ENGER

PERSONAL PRAYER AND REFLECTION

CLOSING PRAYER

And when I rest in glory bright,
The burden of my labor past,
In hymns I'll praise Thee more and more
While the eternal ages last.
—adapted from the poetry of
SYNESIUS (Greek, AD 375–430)

READINGS FOR WEEK 25

A Better Resurrection

CHRISTINA ROSSETTI (English, 1830–1894)

I have no wit, no words, no tears;
  My heart within me like a stone
Is numbed too much for hopes or fears;
  Look right, look left, I dwell alone;
I lift mine eyes, but dimmed with grief
  No everlasting hills I see;
My life is in the falling leaf:
  O Jesus, quicken me.

My life is like a faded leaf,
  My harvest dwindled to a husk;
Truly my life is void and brief
  And tedious in the barren dusk;
My life is like a frozen thing,
  No bud nor greenness can I see:
Yet rise it shall—the sap of Spring;
  O Jesus, rise in me.

My life is like a broken bowl,
  A broken bowl that cannot hold
One drop of water for my soul
  Or cordial in the searching cold;
Cast in the fire the perished thing,
  Melt and remold it, till it be
A royal cup for Him my King:
  O Jesus, drink of me.

———

The Caged Skylark

GERARD MANLEY HOPKINS (English, 1844–1889)

As a dare-gale skylark scanted in a dull cage
 Man's mounting spirit in his bone-house, mean house, dwells—
 That bird beyond the remembering his free fells;
This in drudgery, day-laboring-out life's age.

Though aloft on turf or perch or poor low stage,
 Both sing sometimes the sweetest, sweetest spells,
 Yet both droop deadly sometimes in their cells
Or wring their barriers in bursts of fear or rage.

Not that the sweet-fowl, song-fowl, needs no rest—
Why, hear him, hear him babble and drop down to his nest,
 But his own nest, wild nest, no prison.

Man's spirit will be flesh-bound when found at best,
But uncumbered: meadow-down is not distressed
 For a rainbow footing it nor he for his bones risen.

Resurrection

JOHN DONNE (English, 1572–1631)

Moist with one drop of thy blood, my dry soul
Shall (though she now be in extreme degree
Too stony hard, and yet too fleshly,) be
Freed by that drop, from being starved, hard, or foul,
And life, by this death abled, shall control
Death, whom thy death slew; nor shall to me
Fear of first or last death, bring misery,
If in thy little book my name thou enroll,

Flesh in that long sleep is not putrefied,
But made that there, of which, and for which 'twas;
Nor can by other means be glorified.
May then sin's sleep, and death's soon from me pass,
That waked from both, I again risen may
Salute the last, and everlasting day.

From *Peace Like a River*

Leif Enger (American, contemporary)

[Editor's note: Young Reuben Land, on the point of death after a shoot-out in his front yard, finds himself in a heavenly country where he has a surprising encounter. What is so eloquent about this scene is not his reunion with a loved one but the concrete physicality both of their bodies and of the country they find themselves in—a strong affirmation of the ancient Christian creed that does not divorce the physical from the spiritual, but states, "I believe in the resurrection of the body."]

And now the orchard ended, and a plain reached far ahead to a range of blanched mountains. A stream coursed through this plain, of different personality and purpose than the earlier wide river. A narrow, raucous stream, it flowed upward against the gradient, and mighty fish arched and swam in it, flinging manes of spray. I meant to jump in—wherever this river went I wanted to go—and would've done so had not another figure appeared, running beside the water.

A man in pants. Flapping colorless pants and a shirt, dismal things most strange in this place. He was running upslope by the boisterous stream. Despite the clothes his face was incandescent, and when he saw me he wheeled his arms and came on ever faster. Then history entered me—my own and all the rest of it, more than I could hold, history like a heavy rain—so I knew the man coming along was my father, Jeremiah Land; and all that had happened, himself slipping down the hood of the Ford, Roxanna's hard grip on my shoulder, the air drumming in my ears like bird wings, came back like a mournful story told from ancient days.

He was beside me in moments, stretching out his hands. What cabled strength! I remember wondering what those arms were made for—no mere reward, they had design in them. They had some work to set about. Meantime Dad was laughing—at my arms, which were similarly strong! He sang out, *You're as big as me!* How had I not noticed? We were like two friends, and I saw he was proud of me, that he knew me better than he'd ever thought to and was not dismayed by the knowledge; and even as I wondered at his ageless face, so clear and at home, his eyes owned up to some small regret, for he knew a thing I didn't.

Let's run, he said. It's true both of us were wild to go on. I tell you there is no one who compels as does the master of that country—although badly as I wanted to see him, Dad must've wanted to more, for he shot ahead like a man who sees all that pleases him most stacked beside the finish. I could only be awed at his speed, which was no effort for him; indeed he held back so that we traveled together, he sometimes reaching for my hand, as he'd done a thousand times in the past; and the music and living language swept us forth across the plains until the mountains lay ahead, and up we climbed at a run.

Is it fair to say that country is more real than ours? That its stone is harder, its water more drenching—that the weather itself is alert and not just background? Can you endure a witness to its tactile presence?

WEEK 26

Hints and Guesses

OPENING PRAYER

O my Lord and my God! how stupendous is Thy grandeur! We are like so many foolish peasant lads: we think we know something of Thee, yet it must be comparatively nothing, for there are profound secrets even in ourselves of which we know naught.

—Teresa of Avila (Spanish, 1515–1582)

SCRIPTURES

Psalm 97 | Daniel 2:1–23 | 1 Corinthians 2:1–13 | John 16:16–24

READINGS

"Questions at the Time" by Paul J. Willis
"Flower in the Crannied Wall" by Alfred, Lord Tennyson
"Hide and Seek" by Enuma Okoro
From "They Desire a Better Country (II)" by Christina Rossetti
From *The Golden Key* by George MacDonald

PERSONAL PRAYER AND REFLECTION

CLOSING PRAYER

What has been, shall not only be, but is.
The hues of dreamland, strange and sweet and tender
Are but hint-shadows of full many a splendor
Which the high Parent-love will yet unroll
Before his child's obedient, humble soul.

Ah me, my God, in thee lies every bliss
Whose shadow men go hunting wearily amiss.
—George MacDonald (Scottish, 1824–1905)

READINGS FOR WEEK 26

Questions at the Time

Paul J. Willis (American, contemporary)

Does willow grow by the lake, or does granite?
Does water tremble there, or the sky?
Does the wind blow, or is it the breath
of a bear speaking quietly? Does a cloud

leave this shadow in place, or is it the backside
of God? Which sun could be shining
except itself? What eye of heaven
tasted by the rich, red lip of this horizon?

Flower in the Crannied Wall

Alfred, Lord Tennyson (English, 1809–1892)

Flower in the crannied wall,
I pluck you out of the crannies;—
I hold you here, root and all, in my hand,
Little flower—but if I could understand
What you are, root and all, and all in all,
I should know what God and man is.

Hide and Seek

ENUMA OKORO (Nigerian-American, contemporary)

To learn your name
seems a task I turn to play
of arms outstretched about me.
Trying to catch revelations
in a childish game of toss-up

But you toss about me from all sides
keeping me tripping to simply grasp at you.
And you're seemingly slipping through my fingers
just when I thought I had you.

I thought you knew
my hands were raised in prayer to you.
Babbling my way through discernments I'd designed.
My guesses of how I'd heard you.
But you break down like syllables
each tower I build to reach you.

Have I overstepped my bounds to know you?

Now your precepts seem like a foreign tongue
as you call out to me in psalms and songs.
Changing more rules I thought I knew,
when you hide and I seek
your hiddenness can make me believe
I see you everywhere.

But to keep from merely looking up
is taking me a lifetime.

How is it this keeps me
tossing, tripping, breaking down
trying to catch a word that reveals you?

Your simple repetitions of who you are
gather me up and lose me,
So the source seems lost in echoes.

And these games . . .
Do I imagine that you play?
Are your ways forever not my ways?
It's you who came to seek the lost
And in this fumbling of my limbs and thoughts
Perhaps it's I who've been the stumbling block.

FROM *"They Desire a Better Country (II)"*
CHRISTINA ROSSETTI (English, 1830–1894)

What seekest thou, far in the unknown land?
In hope I follow joy gone on before;
In hope and fear persistent more and more,
As the dry desert lengthens out its sand.
Whilst day and night I carry in my hand
The golden key to ope[21] the golden door
Of golden home; yet mine eye weepeth sore,
For long the journey is that makes no stand.
And who is this that veiled doth walk with thee?
Lo, this is Love that walketh at my right;
One exile holds us both, and we are bound
To selfsame home-joys in the land of light.
Weeping thou walkest with him; weepeth he?—
Some sobbing weep, some weep and make no sound.

---

21 *ope*—shorthand for "open."

FROM *The Golden Key*

GEORGE MACDONALD (Scottish, 1824–1905)

[Editor's note: In MacDonald's haunting fairytale, Mossy and Tangle are on a quest to find the lock that fits the golden key Mossy has found. They find themselves in a valley full of shadows (an echo of Plato's famous cave), which stirs in them a longing to find the country from whence the shadows fall, where the real, solid creatures are to be found. The shadows and the longing hint at a deeper reality beyond what the eye can see.]

Looking down, they could not tell whether the valley below was a grassy plain or a great still lake. They had never seen any space look like it. The way to it was difficult and dangerous, but down the narrow path they went, and reached the bottom in safety. They found it composed of smooth, light-colored sandstone, undulating in parts, but mostly level. It was no wonder to them now that they had not been able to tell what it was, for this surface was everywhere crowded with shadows. It was a sea of shadows. . . .

. . . Now a wonderful form, half bird-like half human, would float across on outspread sailing pinions. Anon an exquisite shadow group of gamboling children would be followed by the loveliest female form, and that again by the grand stride of a Titanic shape, each disappearing in the surrounding press of shadowy foliage. Sometimes a profile of unspeakable beauty or grandeur would appear for a moment and vanish. Sometimes they seemed lovers that passed linked arm in arm, sometimes father and son, sometimes brothers in loving contest, sometimes sisters entwined in gracefullest community of complex form. Sometimes wild horses would tear across, free, or bestrode by noble shadows of ruling men. But some of the things which pleased them most they never knew how to describe.

"We *must* find the country from which the shadows come," said Mossy.

"We must, dear Mossy," responded Tangle. "What if your golden key should be the key to *it*?"

"Ah! that would be grand," returned Mossy.—"But we must rest here for a little, and then we shall be able to cross the plain before night."

So he lay down on the ground, and about him on every side, and over his head, was the constant play of the wonderful shadows. He could look through them, and see the one behind the other, till they mixed in a mass of darkness. Tangle, too, lay admiring, and wondering, and longing after the country whence the shadows came. When they were rested they rose and pursued their journey.

[continued below]

FROM *The Golden Key*

How long they were in crossing this plain I cannot tell; but before night Mossy's hair was streaked with grey, and Tangle had got wrinkles on her forehead.

As evening drew on, the shadows fell deeper and rose higher. At length they reached a place where they rose above their heads, and made all dark around them. Then they took hold of each other's hand, and walked on in silence and in some dismay. They felt the gathering darkness, and something strangely solemn besides, and the beauty of the shadows ceased to delight them. All at once Tangle found that she had not a hold of Mossy's hand, though when she lost it she could not tell.

"Mossy, Mossy!" she cried aloud in terror.

But no Mossy replied.

A moment after, the shadows sank to her feet, and down under her feet, and the mountains rose before her. She turned towards the gloomy region she had left, and called once more upon Mossy. There the gloom lay tossing and heaving, a dark, stormy, foamless sea of shadows, but no Mossy rose out of it, or came climbing up the hill on which she stood. She threw herself down and wept in despair.

Suddenly she remembered that the beautiful lady had told them, if they lost each other in the country of which she could not remember the name, they were not to be afraid, but go straight on.

"And besides," she said to herself, "Mossy has the golden key, and so no harm will come to him, I do believe."

She rose from the ground, and went on.

WEEK 27

Rending the Veil

OPENING PRAYER

Reveal Your presence,
And let the vision and Your beauty kill me,
Behold the malady
Of love is incurable
Except in Your presence and before Your face.
—JOHN OF THE CROSS (Spanish, 1542–1591)

SCRIPTURES

PSALM 24 | EXODUS 3:13–15 | ROMANS 8:18–25 | LUKE 24:13–35

READINGS

"Only in lofty words" by ENUMA OKORO
"The Created" by JONES VERY
From *The Man Who Was Thursday* by G. K. CHESTERTON

PERSONAL PRAYER AND REFLECTION

CLOSING PRAYER

Then shall my heart behold thee everywhere.
The vision rises of a speechless thing,
A perfectness of bliss beyond compare!
A time when I nor breathe nor think nor move,
But I do breathe and think and feel thy love,

The soul of all the songs the saints do sing!
And life dies out in bliss, to come again in prayer.
—George MacDonald (Scottish, 1824–1905)

READINGS FOR WEEK 27

Only in lofty words

Enuma Okoro (Nigerian-American, contemporary)

Only in lofty words
can I explore You
and feel you out like Braille,
reading by seeing hand and mind
the inconspicuous places
right before me.
A poet afraid to touch,
I am,
leafing a way through
all your poems of creation:
Dark earth, distant sky, morning, noon,
and night strung out
line by line.

It's so easy to catch your rhythms and rhymes.
Why can't you be coy,
avoid the overused
"blue sky," "bright stars,"
a head trip to complicate your style,
re-narrate the world in code,
"a rose is a rose?" Oh,
mysterious God, confound me a little,

make my brittle bones believe they're brittle,
exhaust me in running circles I create,
explicate your grace for this intelligent fool.
The wisdom of your world escapes me.

The Created

JONES VERY (American, 1813–1880)

There is naught for thee by thy haste to gain;
'Tis not the swift with Me that win the race;
Through long endurance of delaying pain,
Thine opened eye shall see thy Father's face;
Nor here nor there, where now thy feet would turn,
Thou wilt find Him who ever seeks for thee;
But let obedience quench desires that burn,
And where thou art, thy Father, too, will be.
Behold! as day by day the spirit grows,
Thou see'st by inward light things hid before;
Till what God is, thyself, his image shows;
And thou dost wear the robe that first thou wore,
When bright with radiance from his forming hand
He saw thee Lord of all his creatures stand.

FROM *The Man Who Was Thursday*

G. K. CHESTERTON (English, 1874–1936)

[Editor's note 1: If you have not read *The Man Who Was Thursday* but plan to at some point, you may wish to skip this excerpt, including the following editorial note, as both contain spoilers.]

[Editor's note 2: In this climactic episode, the six members of the Central Council of Anarchists—who all, it turns out, are undercover detectives like Syme—set out to confront the seventh man, their President "Sunday." Their quest to unveil the true identity of their larger-than-life leader takes on spiritual overtones when Sunday refuses to answer their questions. Instead he hints at a larger purpose—indeed, at a larger, almost divine personality—beyond what they can grasp.]

Next morning the battalion of the reunited six marched stolidly towards the hotel in Leicester Square.

"This is more cheerful," said Dr. Bull; "we are six men going to ask one man what he means."

"I think it is a bit queerer than that," said Syme. "I think it is six men going to ask one man what they mean."

They turned in silence into the Square, and, though the hotel was in the opposite corner, they saw at once the little balcony and a figure that looked too big for it. He was sitting alone with bent head, poring over a newspaper. But all his councilors, who had come to vote him down, crossed that Square as if they were watched out of heaven by a hundred eyes.

They had disputed much upon their policy, about whether they should leave the unmasked Gogol without and begin diplomatically, or whether they should bring him in and blow up the gunpowder at once. The influence of Syme and Bull prevailed for the latter course, though the Secretary to the last asked them why they attacked Sunday so rashly.

"My reason is quite simple," said Syme. "I attack him rashly because I am afraid of him."

They followed Syme up the dark stair in silence, and they all came out simultaneously into the broad sunlight of the morning and the broad daylight of Sunday's smile.

"Delightful!" he said. "So pleased to see you all. What an exquisite day it is. Is the Czar dead?"

The Secretary, who happened to be foremost, drew himself together for a dignified outburst.

"No, sir," he said sternly, "there has been no massacre. I bring you news of no such disgusting spectacles."

"Disgusting spectacles?" repeated the President, with a bright, inquiring smile. "You mean Dr. Bull's spectacles?"

The Secretary choked for a moment, and the President went on with a sort of smooth appeal:

"Of course, we all have our opinions and even our eyes, but really to call them disgusting before the man himself—"

Dr. Bull tore off his spectacles and broke them on the table.

"My spectacles are blackguardly," he said, "but I'm not. Look at my face."

"I dare say it's the sort of face that grows on one," said the President, "in fact, it grows on you; and who am I to quarrel with the wild fruits upon the Tree of Life? I dare say it will grow on me some day."

"We have no time for tomfoolery," said the Secretary, breaking in savagely. "We have come to know what all this means. Who are you? What are you? Why did you get us all here? Do you know who and what we are? Are you a half-witted man playing the conspirator, or are you a clever man playing the fool? Answer me, I tell you."

"Candidates," murmured Sunday, "are only required to answer eight out of the seventeen questions on the paper. As far as I can make out, you want me to tell you what I am, and what you are, and what this table is, and what this Council is, and what this world is for all I know. Well, I will go so far as to rend the veil of one mystery. If you want to know what you are, you are a set of highly well-intentioned young jackasses."

"And you," said Syme, leaning forward, "what are you?"

"I? What am I?" roared the President, and he rose slowly to an incredible height, like some enormous wave about to arch above them and break. "You want to know what I am, do you? Bull, you are a man of science. Grub in the roots of those trees and find out the truth about them. Syme, you are a poet. Stare at those morning clouds. But I tell you this, that you will have found out the truth of the last tree and the topmost cloud before the truth about me. You will understand the sea, and I shall be still a riddle; you shall know what the stars are, and not know what I am. Since the beginning of the world all men have hunted me like a wolf—kings and sages, and poets and law-givers, all the churches, and all the philosophers. But I have never been caught yet, and the skies will fall in the time I turn to bay. I have given them a good run for their money, and I will now."

Before one of them could move, the monstrous man had swung himself like some huge orangutan over the balustrade of the balcony. Yet before he dropped he pulled himself up again as on a horizontal bar, and thrusting his great chin over the edge of the balcony, said solemnly:

"There's one thing I'll tell you, though, about who I am. I am the man in the dark room, who made you all policemen."

With that he fell from the balcony, bouncing on the stones below like a great ball of india-rubber, and went bounding towards the corner of the Alhambra, where he hailed a hansom-cab and sprang inside it. The six detectives had been standing thunderstruck and livid in the light of his last assertion: but when he disappeared into the cab, Syme's practical senses returned to him, and leaping over the balcony so recklessly as almost to break his legs, he called another cab.

WEEK 28

Rumors of Another World

OPENING PRAYER

How lovely are thy dwellings fair!
O Lord of Hosts, how dear
The pleasant tabernacles are!
Where thou dost dwell so near.
My soul doth long and almost die
Thy courts O Lord to see;
My heart and flesh aloud do cry,
O living God, for thee.
—JOHN MILTON (English, 1608–1674)

SCRIPTURES

PSALM 42 | GENESIS 28:10–22 | HEBREWS 12:18–29 | JOHN 8:21–30

READINGS

"At the Border of Paradise" by ANNA KAMIEŃSKA
"At a Solemn Music" by JOHN MILTON
"Peace" by HENRY VAUGHAN
From "They Desire a Better Country (III)" by CHRISTINA ROSSETTI
From "The Passing of Arthur" in *Idylls of the King* by ALFRED, LORD TENNYSON
"Crossing the Bar" by ALFRED, LORD TENNYSON

PERSONAL PRAYER AND REFLECTION

CLOSING PRAYER

Ever the richest, tenderest glow
  Sets round the autumnal sun—
But there sight fails: no heart may know
  The bliss when life is done.

Such is Thy banquet, dearest Lord;
  O give us grace, to cast
Our lot with Thine, to trust Thy word,
  And keep our best till last.
—JOHN KEBLE (English, 1792–1866)

READINGS FOR WEEK 28

At the Border of Paradise

ANNA KAMIEŃSKA (Polish, 1920–1986)

It's strange
that green valleys are still here
as if happiness slept in them
and shady streams
we once knew for sure
existed
and that there still are roofs
under which small children sleep
filling the house with a different silence

It's strange
that clouds here still follow the sun
like gliding birds
and that there still is simple human goodness
besides what aspires upwards

that pure music stands at the door
which suddenly seems like a palace portico

It's strange
that we still
want so much to love and cry

At a Solemn Music

JOHN MILTON (English, 1608–1674)

Blest pair of sirens, pledges of Heaven's joy,
Sphere-borne harmonious sisters, Voice and Verse,
Wed your divine sounds, and mixed power employ
Dead things with inbreathed sense able to pierce,
And to our high-raised fantasy present
That undisturbèd song of pure consent,
Ay sung before the sapphire-colored throne
To him that sits thereon
With saintly shout, and solemn jubilee,
Where the bright Seraphim in burning row
Their loud uplifted angel trumpets blow,
And the Cherubic host in thousand choirs
Touch their immortal harps of golden wires,
With those just spirits that wear victorious palms,
Hymns devout and holy psalms
Singing everlastingly;
That we on earth with undiscording voice
May rightly answer that melodious noise;
As once we did, till disproportioned sin
Jarred against nature's chime, and with harsh din
Broke the fair music that all creatures made

To their great Lord, whose love their motion swayed
In perfect diapason, whilst they stood
In first obedience, and their state of good.
O may we soon again renew that song,
And keep in tune with Heav'n, till God ere long
To his celestial consort us unite,
To live with him, and sing in endless morn of light.

Peace

HENRY VAUGHAN (Welsh, 1622–1695)

My soul, there is a country
  Far beyond the stars,
Where stands a wingèd sentry
  All skillful in the wars.
There, above noise and danger,
  Sweet peace sits crowned with smiles,
And one born in a manger
  Commands the beauteous files.[22]
He is thy gracious friend
  And (O my soul, awake!)
Did in pure love descend
  To die here for thy sake.
If thou canst get but thither,
  There grows the flower of peace,
The rose that cannot wither,
  Thy fortress, and thy ease.
Leave then thy foolish ranges;
  For none can thee secure

22 *files*—archaic usage of "crowds," e.g., rank and file soldier.

But one, who never changes,
  Thy God, thy life, thy cure.

FROM *"They Desire a Better Country (III)"*
CHRISTINA ROSSETTI (English, 1830–1894)

A dimness of a glory glimmers here
  Thro' veils and distance from the space remote,
  A faintest far vibration of a note
Reaches to us and seems to bring us near;
Causing our face to glow with braver cheer,
  Making the serried mist to stand afloat,
  Subduing languor with an antidote,
And strengthening love almost to cast out fear:
Till for one moment golden city walls
  Rise looming on us, golden walls of home,
Light of our eyes until the darkness falls;
  Then thro' the outer darkness burdensome
I hear again the tender voice that calls,
  "Follow me hither, follow, rise, and come."

FROM "The Passing of Arthur" in *Idylls of the King*
ALFRED, LORD TENNYSON (English, 1809–1892)

[Editor's note: King Arthur lies dying from an incurable wound; and, mourned by the last remaining knight of the Round Table, Sir Bedivere, Arthur is placed upon a floating barge that will be pushed out to sea. As the barge disappears from sight, Bedivere is given a vision, if only a glimpse, of the distant Avalon, the immortal, life-giving island of legend where the barge presumably lands. It is a poignant scene expressing the longing of a disciple for the lord who has gone to a better country—and the disciple's hope that the lord will one day return.]

Then loudly cried the bold Sir Bedivere:
"Ah! my Lord Arthur, whither shall I go?
Where shall I hide my forehead and my eyes?
For now I see the true old times are dead,
When every morning brought a noble chance,
And every chance brought out a noble knight.
Such times have been not since the light that led
The holy Elders with the gift of myrrh.
But now the whole Round Table is dissolved
Which was an image of the mighty world,
And I, the last, go forth companionless,
And the days darken round me, and the years,
Among new men, strange faces, other minds."

And slowly answered Arthur from the barge:
"The old order changeth, yielding place to new,
And God fulfils himself in many ways,
Lest one good custom should corrupt the world.
Comfort thyself: what comfort is in me?
I have lived my life, and that which I have done
May He within himself make pure! but thou,
If thou shouldst never see my face again,
Pray for my soul. More things are wrought by prayer
Than this world dreams of. Wherefore, let thy voice
Rise like a fountain for me night and day.
For what are men better than sheep or goats
That nourish a blind life within the brain,
If, knowing God, they lift not hands of prayer

Both for themselves and those who call them friend?
For so the whole round earth is every way
Bound by gold chains about the feet of God.
But now farewell. I am going a long way
With these thou seest—if indeed I go
(For all my mind is clouded with a doubt)—
To the island-valley of Avilion;
Where falls not hail, or rain, or any snow,
Nor ever wind blows loudly; but it lies
Deep-meadowed, happy, fair with orchard lawns
And bowery hollows crowned with summer sea,
Where I will heal me of my grievous wound."

So said he, and the barge with oar and sail
Moved from the brink, like some full-breasted swan
That, fluting a wild carol ere her death,
Ruffles her pure cold plume, and takes the flood
With swarthy webs. Long stood Sir Bedivere
Revolving many memories, till the hull
Looked one black dot against the verge of dawn,
And on the mere the wailing died away.

[continued below]

FROM *"The Passing of Arthur"*

But when that moan had past for evermore,
The stillness of the dead world's winter dawn
Amazed him, and he groaned, "The King is gone."
And therewithal came on him the weird rhyme,
"From the great deep to the great deep he goes."

Whereat he slowly turned and slowly clomb[23]
The last hard footstep of that iron crag;
Thence marked the black hull moving yet, and cried,
"He passes to be King among the dead,
And after healing of his grievous wound
He comes again; but—if he come no more—
O me, be yon dark Queens in yon black boat,
Who shrieked and wailed, the three whereat we gazed
On that high day, when, clothed with living light,
They stood before his throne in silence, friends
Of Arthur, who should help him at his need?"

Then from the dawn it seemed there came, but faint
As from beyond the limit of the world,
Like the last echo born of a great cry,
Sounds, as if some fair city were one voice
Around a king returning from his wars.

Thereat once more he moved about, and clomb
Even to the highest he could climb, and saw,
Straining his eyes beneath an arch of hand,
Or thought he saw, the speck that bare the King,
Down that long water opening on the deep
Somewhere far off, pass on and on, and go
From less to less and vanish into light.
And the new sun rose bringing the new year.

---

23 *clomb*—archaic word for "climbed."

Crossing the Bar

Alfred, Lord Tennyson (English, 1809–1892)

Sunset and evening star,
  And one clear call for me!
And may there be no moaning of the bar,
  When I put out to sea,

But such a tide as moving seems asleep,
  Too full for sound and foam,
When that which drew from out the boundless deep
  Turns again to home.

Twilight and evening bell,
  And after that the dark!
And may there be no sadness of farewell,
  When I embark;

For though from out our bourne[24] of Time and Place
  The flood may bear me far,
I hope to see my Pilot face to face
When I have crossed the bar.

24 *bourne*—goal or destination.

WEEK 29

All Shall Be Well

OPENING PRAYER

Heaven is not far, though far the sky
  Overarching earth and main.
It takes not long to live and die,
  Die, revive, and rise again.
Not long: how long? Oh, long re-echoing song!
  O Lord, how long?
—Christina Rossetti (English, 1830–1894)

SCRIPTURES

Psalm 23 | Isaiah 11:1–9 | Revelation 21:1–27 | John 14:1–7

READINGS

"Eschaton" by Elizabeth B. Rooney
"All shall be well" by Julian of Norwich
"Rinsed with Gold, Endless, Walking the Fields" by Robert Siegel
From *The Pilgrim's Progress* by John Bunyan

PERSONAL PRAYER AND REFLECTION

CLOSING BENEDICTION

And all shall be well and
All manner of thing shall be well.
—T. S. Eliot (American-English, 1888–1965)

READINGS FOR WEEK 29

Eschaton

ELIZABETH B. ROONEY (American, 1924–1999)

I saw the world end yesterday!
A flight of angels tore
Its cover off and Heaven lay
Where earth had been before.

I walked about the countryside
And saw a cricket pass.
Then, bending closer, I espied
An ecstasy of grass.

All shall be well

(ADAPTED FROM *Revelations of Divine Love*)
JULIAN OF NORWICH (English, ca. 1342–ca. 1416)

And so our good Lord answered
  to all the questions and doubts
    that I might make,
  saying comfortingly:
    I may make all thing well,
    I can make all thing well,
    I will make all thing well,
    and I shall make all thing well;
    and thou shall see thyself
    that all manner of thing shall be well.

Where He says, *I may,*
  I understand it for the Father;
and where He says, *I can,*
  I understand it for the Son;
and where He says, *I will,*
  I understand it for the Holy Ghost;
and where He says, *I shall,*
  I understand it for the unity of the blessed Trinity:
    three Persons and one Truth;
and where He says, *Thou shall see thy self,*
  I understand the oneing of all mankind
    that shall be saved unto the blessed Trinity.
  And in these five words
    God wills we be enclosed
      in rest and in peace.

Rinsed with Gold, Endless, Walking the Fields

ROBERT SIEGEL (American, contemporary)

Let this day's air praise the Lord—
Rinsed with gold, endless, walking the fields,
Blue and bearing the clouds like censers,
Holding the sun like a single note
Running through all things, a *basso profundo*[25]
Rousing the birds to an endless chorus.

Let the river throw itself down before him,
The rapids laugh and flash with his praise,
Let the lake tremble about its edges
And gather itself in one clear thought

25 *basso profundo*—the lowest bass voice.

To mirror the heavens and the reckless gulls
That swoop and rise on its glittering shores.

Let the lawn burn continually before him
A green flame, and the tree's shadow
Sweep over it like the baton of a conductor,
Let winds hug the housecorners and woodsmoke
Sweeten the world with her invisible dress,
Let the cricket wind his heartspring
And draw the night by like a child's toy.

Let the tree stand and thoughtfully consider
His presence as its leaves dip and row
The long sea of winds, as sun and moon
Unfurl and decline like contending flags.

Let blackbirds quick as knives praise the Lord,
Let the sparrow line the moon for her nest
And pick the early sun for her cherry,
Let her slide on the outgoing breath of evening,
Telling of raven and dove,
The quick flutters, homings to the green houses.

Let the worm climb a winding stair,
Let the mole offer no sad explanation
As he paddles aside the dark from his nose,
Let the dog tug on the leash of his bark,
The startled cat electrically hiss,
And the snake sign her name in the dust

In joy. For it is he who underlies
The rock from its liquid foundation,
The sharp contraries of the giddy atom,
The unimaginable curve of space,
Time pulling like a patient string,

And gravity, fiercest of natural loves.

At his laughter, splendor riddles the night,
Galaxies swarm from a secret hive,
Mountains split and crawl for aeons
To huddle again, and planets melt
In the last tantrum of a dying star.

At his least signal spring shifts
Its green patina over half the earth,
Deserts whisper themselves over cities,
Polar caps widen and wither like flowers.

In his stillness rock shifts, root probes,
The spider tenses her geometrical ego,
The larva dreams in the heart of the peachwood,
The child's pencil makes a shaky line,
The dog sighs and settles deeper,
And a smile takes hold like the feet of a bird.

Sit straight, let the air ride down your backbone,
Let your lungs unfold like a field of roses,
Your eyes hang the sun and moon between them,
Your hands weigh the sky in even balance,
Your tongue, swiftest of members, release a word
Spoken at conception to the sanctum of genes,
And each breath rise sinuous with praise.

Let your feet move to the rhythm of your pulse
(Your joints like pearls and rubies he has hidden),
And your hands float high on the tide of your feelings.
Now, shout from the stomach, hoarse with music,
Give gladness and joy back to the Lord,
Who, sly as a milkweed, takes root in your heart.

FROM *The Pilgrim's Progress*
JOHN BUNYAN (English, 1628–1688)

[Editor's note: Bunyan's classic allegory finally brings Christian and his companion, Hopeful, within sight of the heavenly city. After many struggles and detours, the way has become easier and more delightful—until the final trial, which is the hardest of all. And yet even as the waters of death close over his head, Christian is given reassurance that all shall be well.]

Now I saw in my dream, that by this time the pilgrims were got over the Enchanted Ground, and entering into the country of Beulah, whose air was very sweet and pleasant, the way lying directly through it, they solaced themselves there for a season. Yea, here they heard continually the singing of birds, and saw every day the flowers appear in the earth, and heard the voice of the turtle in the land. In this country the sun shineth night and day: wherefore this was beyond the Valley of the Shadow of Death, and also out of the reach of Giant Despair; neither could they from this place so much as see Doubting Castle. Here they were within sight of the city they were going to; also here met them some of the inhabitants thereof; for in this land the shining ones commonly walked, because it was upon the borders of heaven. In this land also the contract between the Bride and the Bridegroom was renewed; yea, here, "as the bridegroom rejoiceth over the bride, so doth God rejoice over them." Here they had no want of corn and wine; for in this place they met with abundance of what they had sought for in all their pilgrimage. Here they heard voices from out of the city, loud voices, saying, "Say ye to the daughter of Zion, Behold, thy salvation cometh! Behold, his reward is with him!" Here all the inhabitants of the country called them "the holy People, the redeemed of the Lord, sought out," etc.

Now, as they walked in this land, they had more rejoicing than in parts more remote from the kingdom to which they were bound; and drawing near to the city, they had yet a more perfect view thereof: It was builded of pearls and precious stones, also the streets thereof were paved with gold; so that, by reason of the natural glory of the city, and the reflection of the sunbeams upon it, Christian with desire fell sick; Hopeful also had a fit or two of the same disease: wherefore here they lay by it a while, crying out because of their pangs, "If you see my Beloved, tell him that I am sick of love."

But, being a little strengthened, and better able to bear their sickness, they walked on their way, and came yet nearer and nearer, where were orchards, vineyards, and gardens, and their gates opened into the highway. Now, as they came up to these places, behold the gardener stood in the way; to whom the pilgrims said, "Whose goodly vineyards and gardens are these?" He answered, "They are the King's, and are planted here for his own delight, and also for the solace of pilgrims." So the gardener had them into the vineyards, and bid them refresh themselves with the dainties. He also showed them there the King's walks, and arbors where he delighted to be: and here they tarried and slept.

[continued below]

FROM *The Pilgrim's Progress*

Now I beheld in my dream, that they talked more in their sleep at this time than ever they did in all their journey; and, being in a muse thereabout, the gardener said even to me, "Wherefore musest thou at the matter? It is the nature of the fruit of the grapes of these vineyards, 'to go down so sweetly as to cause the lips of them that are asleep to speak.'"

So I saw that when they awoke, they addressed themselves to go up to the city. But, as I said, the reflection of the sun upon the city (for the city was pure gold) was so extremely glorious, that they could not as yet with open face behold it, but through an instrument made for that purpose. So I saw, that as they went on, there met them two men in raiment that shone like gold, also their faces shone as the light.

These men asked the pilgrims whence they came; and they told them. They also asked them where they had lodged, what difficulties and dangers, what comforts and pleasures, they had met with in the way; and they told them. Then said the men that met them, "You have but two difficulties more to meet with, and then you are in the City."

Christian then and his companion asked the men to go along with them: so they told them that they would. "But," said they, "you must obtain it by your own faith." So I saw in my dream, that they went on together till they came in sight of the gate.

Now I further saw, that betwixt them and the gate was a river; but there was no bridge to go over, and the river was very deep. At the sight, therefore, of this river the pilgrims were much stunned; but the men that went with them said, "You must go through, or you cannot come at the gate."

The pilgrims then began to inquire if there was no other way to the gate. To which they answered, "Yes; but there hath not any, save two, to wit, Enoch and Elijah, been permitted to tread that path since the foundation of the world, nor shall until the last trumpet shall sound." The pilgrims then, especially Christian, began to despond in their mind, and looked this way and that, but no way could be found by them by which they might escape the river. Then they asked the men if the waters were all of a depth. They said, "No"; yet they could not help them in that case; for, said they, "You shall find it deeper or shallower as you believe in the King of the place."

Then they addressed themselves to the water, and entering, Christian began to sink, and crying out to his good friend Hopeful, he said, "I sink in deep waters; the billows go over my head; all his waves go over me. Selah."

Then said the other, "Be of good cheer, my brother: I feel the bottom, and it is good."

CLOSING THOUGHTS

After twenty-nine weeks of changing seasons and roaming thoughts, we have come to the end of Ordinary Time. The days are shorter now. Creatures have taken flight or burrowed underground. Tomorrow Advent begins. Poets and writers have walked alongside us during these ordinary days; now we turn to prophets and angels, minstrels and magi. And perhaps we are ready, ready for the light shining in the darkness, ready to receive the one whose mystery we have explored in all its aspects for the past seven months. May you enter Advent with an imagination well nourished and a prayer life deepened by the readings you encountered during Ordinary Time.

FOR FURTHER READING

Many of the following works were read or consulted during the creation of this anthology. Though not an exhaustive list, it offers a jumping-off point for deeper exploration of the themes. As some of the works are more pertinent to certain themes than others, I have given suggested weeks during Ordinary Time when you might read them alongside the materials printed in this book. You'll note that some of the works are listed under more than one theme.

Week 1 *Encountering the Spirit*

- The poem "Poet: Silent After Pentecost" from *Polishing the Petoskey Stone* by Luci Shaw
- The poem "Passage" from *Oblique Prayers* by Denise Levertov

Week 2 *In the Stillness*

- The poem "Burnt Norton (II)" from the poem cycle *Four Quartets* by T. S. Eliot
- The novel *Gilead* by Marilynne Robinson
- Selected poems from Wendell Berry's *Sabbaths*

Week 3 *The Other Side of Silence*

- "My period had come for prayer—" from *The Complete Poems of Emily Dickinson*

Week 4 *Seeking God's Face*

- Selected poems from *Thirst* by Mary Oliver, including "Praying"

Week 5 *The Intimacy of Grace*

- Selected entries (especially the later ones) from Sarah Miles's diary in the novel *The End of the Affair* by Graham Greene
- "At least—to pray—is left—is left" from *The Complete Poems of Emily Dickinson*

Week 6 *Sharing Burdens*

- The novel *A Prayer for Owen Meany* by John Irving
- "Prayer (2)" from *The Collected Poems of Langston Hughes*

Week 7 *Ask, Seek, Knock*

- The novel *The Scent of Water* by Elizabeth Goudge. Note: Most of Goudge's novels are out of print, but you may be able to find copies at libraries or used bookstores. She is well worth discovering.
- "Prayer (1)" from *The Collected Poems of Langston Hughes*

Week 8 *Quarrels with Heaven*

- "There comes an hour when begging stops" from *The Complete Poems of Emily Dickinson*
- The novel *A Song I Knew by Heart* by Bret Lott
- The novel *Till We Have Faces* by C. S. Lewis

Week 9 *Dark Night*

- Selected poems in *Book of My Nights* by Li-Young Lee

Week 10 *A Haunted Conscience*

- The short story "The Minister's Black Veil" by Nathaniel Hawthorne

- The novel *All Hallows' Eve* by Charles Williams
- The novella *Notes from Underground* by Fyodor Dostoevsky

Week 11 *Unexpected Encounter*

- The short story "The Blue Cross" from *The Innocence of Father Brown* by G. K. Chesterton
- The novel *Angel Time* by Anne Rice

Week 12 *Cry from the Depths*

- "Feet o' Jesus" from *The Collected Poems of Langston Hughes*
- *Robinson Crusoe* by Daniel Defoe

Week 13 *Compelled by Mercy*

- The poems "The Scarecrow" and "The Burning Glass" from *The Burning Glass* by Walter de la Mare
- The novel *Brideshead Revisited* by Evelyn Waugh

Week 14 *Ransomed for Good*

- The allegory *The Pilgrim's Progress: Part Two* by John Bunyan (the story of Christian's wife, Christiana)

Week 15 *Bending the Knee*

- The poem "The Prodigal" from *The Complete Poems: 1927–1979* by Elizabeth Bishop
- The poem "Repentance" by George Herbert

Week 16 *Fresh Vision*

- The poem "The Dawning" by George Herbert

Week 17 *Called by God*

- Selected poems from *Oblique Prayers* by Denise Levertov, including "St. Peter and the Angel"

Week 18 *The Harder Road*

- The allegory *The Pilgrim's Regress* by C. S. Lewis

Week 19 *Put to the Test*

- The novel *Blue Shoe* by Anne Lamott
- The fairytale "A Lost Paradise" by Andrew Lang

Week 20 *Growing Good*

- The novel *Saint Maybe* by Anne Tyler
- The poem "Making the House Ready for the Lord" from *Thirst* by Mary Oliver
- The short story "The Coming of the King" from *The Golden Windows* by Laura E. Richards

Week 21 *Communion of the Body*

- The novel *Godric* by Frederick Buechner
- The poem "As I walked out one evening" (38) from *Selected Poems* by W. H. Auden

Week 22 *Cloud of Witnesses*

- The novel *The Chosen* by Chaim Potok

Week 23 *In God's House*

- The novel *Gilead* by Marilynne Robinson

Week 24 *It Is Finished*

- The death of Lord Marchmain in *Brideshead Revisited* by Evelyn Waugh
- The novel *Charming Billy* by Alice McDermott
- The poem "Little Round" from *Book of My Nights* by Li-Young Lee

Week 25 *A Better Resurrection*

- "'And with what body do they come?'—" from *The Complete Poems of Emily Dickinson*
- The poem "What good shall my life do me?" by Christina Rossetti

Week 26 *Hints and Guesses*

- The poem "The Dry Salvages (V)" from the poem cycle *Four Quartets* by T. S. Eliot
- The poem "Filling Station" from *The Complete Poems: 1927–1979* by Elizabeth Bishop

Week 27 *Rending the Veil*

- The novel *The Place of the Lion* by Charles Williams

Week 28 *Rumors of Another World*

- The poems "This world is not conclusion" and "Life—is what—we make it—" from *The Complete Poems of Emily Dickinson*

Week 29 *All Shall Be Well*

- The poem "Little Gidding (V)" from the poem cycle *Four Quartets* by T. S. Eliot

ACKNOWLEDGMENTS AND PERMISSIONS

Many thanks to Lauren Winner and Jon Sweeney for reminding me, in the depths of divinity school, that my primary calling is to be a writer. Thanks also to my literary friends—especially Jami Blaauw-Hara, Andrew Cuneo, Liz DeGaynor, Enuma Okoro, Christy Polk, Laura Schmidt, Amy Scott, and Michael Ward—for their helpful input on which authors and poets I should include. To my father, Reverend Bob Faulman, for suggesting *lectio divina* as a model for reading literature meditatively; and Dr. J. Warren Smith of Duke Divinity School for providing last-minute Latin expertise. And of course to my husband, Tom, who selflessly gave up his *really comfy* office chair so his pregnant wife could keep typing. But above all, to the "Primary Imagination" (in Coleridge's words), who over the centuries has inspired writers to express the inexpressible, here at the still point, where words so often fail.

Acknowledgment is gratefully made for permission to include the following works or excerpts:

CAIRNS, SCOTT: selected poems from *Compass of Affection: Poems New and Selected*. Copyright 2006 by Scott Cairns. Used by permission of Paraclete Press: http://www.paracletepress.com

ENGER, LEIF: excerpts from *Peace Like a River*. Copyright 2001 by Leif Enger. Used by permission of Grove/Atlantic, Inc.

JARMAN, MARK: "As the couple turn toward each other" from *Epistles*. Copyright 2007 by Mark Jarman. Reprinted with the permission of Sarabande Books, www.sarabandebooks.org.

KAMIEŃSKA, ANNA: selected poems from *Astonishments: Selected Poems of Anna Kamieńska*. Copyright 2007 by Pawel Śpiewak. Translation and compilation copyright 2007 by Grażyna Drabik and David Curzon. Used by permission of Paraclete Press: http://www.paracletepress.com.

KEILLOR, GARRISON: excerpt from *Lake Wobegon Days*. Copyright 1985 by Garrison Keillor. Used by permission of Viking Penguin, a division of Penguin Group (USA) Inc.

NORRIS, KATHLEEN: "Hester Prynne Recalls a Sunday in June"; "The Companionable Dark"; and Part II of "Little Girls in Church" from *Little Girls in Church*. Copyright 1995 by Kathleen Norris. Reprinted by permission of the University of Pittsburgh Press.

OKORO, ENUMA: "Passing Ordinary Time"; "Morning Reflections"; "Reflections on 'A Certain Woman'"; "Hide and Seek"; and "Only in lofty words." Copyright Enuma Okoro. Used by permission of the author: http://www.enumaokoro.com.

PATERSON, KATHERINE: excerpt from *Jacob Have I Loved*. Copyright 1980 by Katherine Paterson. Used by permission of HarperCollins Publishers.

PRATT, MARY F. C.: "Not Like a Dove." Copyright Mary F. C. Pratt. First published in *The Other Side* (Spring 2003) and *Behold: Arts for the Church Year* (Lent–Easter 2006). Used by permission of the author: http://gladerrand.wordpress.com.

———: "Cathedral Windows." Copyright Mary F. C. Pratt. First published in *The Penwood Review* (October 2007). Used by permission of the author: http://gladerrand.wordpress.com.

RECINOS, HAROLD J.: "Speak." Copyright Harold J. Recinos. Previously printed in *Weavings: A Journal of the Christian Spiritual Life* (July/August 2008) and *Good News from the Barrio: Prophetic Witness for the Church*, by Harold J. Recinos (Westminster John Knox Press, 2005). Used by permission of the author.

ROONEY, ELIZABETH B.: "Eschaton" and "Mute" from *All Miracle: Packages*. Copyright 2001 by the Elizabeth B. Rooney Family Trust. Used by permission of the Elizabeth B. Rooney Family Trust. http://www.brighamfarm.com.

SIEGEL, ROBERT: selected poems from *A Pentecost of Finches: New and Selected Poems*. Copyright 2006 by Robert Siegel. Used by permission of Paraclete Press: http://www.paracletepress.com.

SHAW, LUCI: "Subliminal messages"; "The foolishness of God"; and "Bethany Chapel." Copyright Luci Shaw. Used by permission of the author: http://www.lucishaw.com.

WILLIS, PAUL J.: "Faith of Our Fathers." Copyright 2003 by Paul J. Willis. First serial publication in *New Song* (Volume 7, no. 1, 2003); published subsequently in *Rosing from the Dead* (WordFarm, 2009). Used with permission from WordFarm.

———: "Questions at the Time." Copyright 2009 by Paul J. Willis. Published in *Rosing from the Dead* (WordFarm, 2009). Used with permission from WordFarm.

Every effort has been made to obtain permission for reprinting or publishing copyrighted material in this book. All other selections are in the public domain or were made according to generally accepted fair-use standards and practices. Should any attribution be found to be incorrect, please send written documentation to the publisher supporting corrections for future printings.

INDEX OF AUTHORS AND SOURCES

INDEX OF SCRIPTURES

ABOUT PARACLETE PRESS

Who We Are

Paraclete Press is a publisher of books, recordings, and DVDs on Christian spirituality. Our publishing represents a full expression of Christian belief and practice—from Catholic to Evangelical, from Protestant to Orthodox.

We are the publishing arm of the Community of Jesus, an ecumenical monastic community in the Benedictine tradition. As such, we are uniquely positioned in the marketplace without connection to a large corporation and with informal relationships to many branches and denominations of faith.

What We Are Doing

Books

Paraclete publishes books that show the richness and depth of what it means to be Christian. Although Benedictine spirituality is at the heart of all that we do, we publish books that reflect the Christian experience across many cultures, time periods, and houses of worship. We publish books that nourish the vibrant life of the church and its people—books about spiritual practice, formation, history, ideas, and customs.

We have several different series, including the best-selling Paraclete Essentials and Paraclete Giants series of classic texts in contemporary English; A Voice from the Monastery—men and women monastics writing about living a spiritual life today; award-winning literary faith fiction and poetry; and the Active Prayer Series that brings creativity and liveliness to any life of prayer.

Recordings

From Gregorian chant to contemporary American choral works, our music recordings celebrate sacred choral music through the centuries. Paraclete distributes the recordings of the internationally acclaimed choir Gloriæ Dei Cantores, praised for their "rapt and fathomless spiritual intensity" by *American Record Guide,* and the Gloriæ Dei Cantores Schola, which specializes in the study and performance of Gregorian chant. Paraclete is also the exclusive North American distributor of the recordings of the Monastic Choir of St. Peter's Abbey in Solesmes, France, long considered to be a leading authority on Gregorian chant.

DVDs

Our DVDs offer spiritual help, healing, and biblical guidance for life issues: grief and loss, marriage, forgiveness, anger management, facing death, and spiritual formation.